Shrimpboat and Gym Bags

Shrimpboat and Gym Bags

SHERI COOPER SINYKIN

Atheneum 1990 New York

My special thanks to Peter Roop, for insights in the beginning; to Phyllis Kauten, Lyn Miller-Lachmann, Winnie Stewart Smeltzer, and Joan Zeier, for support along the way; to Sharyn November and Gail Paris, for editorial guidance; and to my husband, Daniel, and sons Rudi and Joshua, for the gift of time.

Atheneum
Macmillan Publishing Company
866 Third Avenue
New York, New York 10022
Collier Macmillan Canada, Inc.

Designed by Kimberly M. Hauck
First Edition
Printed in the United States of America
10 9 8 7 6 5 4 3 2 1

Library of Congress Cataloging-in-Publication Data
Sinykin, Sheri Cooper.
Shrimpboat and gym bags / Sheri Cooper Sinykin. — 1st ed.
p. cm.
Summary: Bo copes with the pressures of moving from California to Wisconsin, keeping his grades up so that he can remain on the gymnastics team, and competing against a talented but temperamental teammate. Includes a glossary of gymnastics terms and information on competitive boys' gymnastics.
ISBN 0-689-31567-8
[1. Gymnastics—Fiction. 2. Moving, Household—Fiction.]
I. Title. PZ7.S6194Sh 1990 [Fic]—dc20 89-34970 CIP AC

My first for my first—
to Aaron, with love

Contents

1

New Boy Blues

BO RAGATZ MADE a heavy pencil slash through "If I Were a Color." Maybe he'd try Idea Number Two. But he could barely see it, seated as he was in the rear of the classroom. Kneeling on his chair, he squinted at the blackboard.

In his best cursive he wrote a new title, "Guess Who I Am."

Yeah, guess, Bo thought. He bit off his eraser. He squirmed in his seat. He caught Mrs. Slater staring at him over the top of her round, black glasses.

"Ahem," she said.

Bo looked at his almost-blank paper. This had to be good. No. Great. The best essay ever. It had to be the one Mrs. Slater chose to read aloud to the class.

"Aha! I've got it!" He clapped his hand—too late—over his mouth.

Everyone laughed.

Bo didn't know why he stood up and bowed. He'd never have done that at his old school. That was for sure. He'd have been too shy. But here, he realized, he could be anything he wanted to be. Even a whole new Bo! It was a giddy feeling.

"You," Mrs. Slater said, and glanced at her seating chart, "sit down and get to work!"

Everyone stopped laughing. Bo's cheeks burned as he shrank back into his chair. Well, at least the kids knew he wasn't a goody-goody. *It was worth it,* he thought as he bent over his paper.

Getting to work wasn't hard, now that he had the Idea. Mrs. Slater would see that he wasn't really a goof-off. Bo would make sure of that.

This is what he wrote:

I am as short as my name. No one believes I'm eleven and four months, especialy since my teeth are just now *starting to come in next to my two front ones. At this rate I'll still have baby teeth when I'm in high school! I wish I could be tall like my brother Christopher. He is almost four but you* ~~wood~~ *would never know it. Everyone thinks he's already in kindergarten. I have straight brown hair and blue eyes. In the summer I have freckles. Red is my faverite color. I hate green food and sharing a room with my brother. I'm glad I only have to do it until my new bedroom set comes. Sometimes Christopher is cute but mostly he's a pain. I am on the boys' gym team and I'm going to win a gold medal. I will really be tall when I get up on that winner stand! We just moved to Madison from California. In my old school I had lots of friends. Nobody knows me here. Who am I?*

Bo stretched his fingers and wished sixth graders were still allowed to print. All that cursive took forever. Rereading the essay, he wondered if he had said too much. He just wanted the kids to know him. No, to like him. He didn't want them to feel sorry for him. That was for sure.

"Psst!" hissed the boy across the aisle. Ever since school had started four days ago, he'd been wearing that same red T-shirt. It boasted a cocky little cartoon animal that looked ready to punch someone's lights out, and MATTHEW spelled out in big, fuzzy letters. "Hey! Yeah, you! How do you spell *goalie*? Y or *i-e*?"

"*I-e*, I think." Bo stared at the cartoon raccoon or tiger or whatever it was. Maybe the *W* on its chest stood for Wisconsin.

"What's the matter?" Matthew said. "Haven't you ever seen Bucky Badger before? Where you from, anyway? Mars?"

Bo shook his head. "Sacramento," he mumbled. "And my name's Bo."

"*B-O?* That's it?" Matthew whispered. "That's your whole name?"

"That's it." Bo wasn't about to explain that Mom had named him after some dumb soap-opera star.

Matthew snorted. "That's a good one. Get it? *Body odor?* You're really funny, you know that?" Matthew wasn't whispering anymore.

The girl in front of Bo started giggling. It was catching. Bo figured only two people *weren't* laughing— him and Mrs. Slater. He slid way down in his seat and tried to look interested in his essay.

But he could hear Mrs. Slater's high heels clacking toward him. Her woodsy perfume tickled his nose. He tried not to sneeze. Slowly, he raised his eyes to meet hers.

"Are you finished?" Mrs. Slater asked.

Bo nodded and handed her his paper.

"I meant you and Matthew. Are you quite finished?"

"I wasn't—"

"Bo's just so *funny,* Mrs. Slater," Matthew cut in. "I didn't mean to laugh, but I couldn't help it."

Chairs creaked as the other kids turned around to stare. The tips of Bo's ears burned. He wished he could crawl inside his desk and disappear forever. This was definitely *not* the new Bo he wanted to be!

"That's twice you've disrupted this class," Mrs. Slater said. "I hope it won't happen again."

"All I did was spell my name. *B-O*. That's all I said!"

Matthew snickered and Mrs. Slater told him to step out in the hall.

Bo wished she'd go back to her desk. He didn't like her towering over him. Especially with that angry look on her face.

But she didn't go. Instead, she picked up his paper, and within moments, the lines around her eyes softened. "This is quite good, Bo, really," she said, penciling in the correct spelling of *especialy* and *faverite*. "Do you mind if I share it with the class?"

"No, go ahead." It was happening! It really was! Once everyone heard his essay, he wouldn't be just "the new boy" anymore. He drummed excitedly on his desk.

"I take it you like that idea," Mrs. Slater said, laying her hand over his. "Think you can hold on until after lunch?" For the first time all day, she actually smiled.

Lunch. If it was going to be anything like yesterday, Bo thought, he might as well stay in and do something useful. Like his homework, maybe. There was nothing worse than standing around by himself with nothing to do.

But once he'd eaten his pizza, the teacher on duty made it clear that stopping at his locker or ducking into the library was out of the question. Bo scowled as he headed toward the playground.

Maybe if he walked slowly enough, he could waste half of recess just getting outside. After all, this wasn't like his old school. There at Erlewine, since the classrooms and cafeteria were in separate, unconnected wings, the playground was as close as the nearest door. Here at Orchard Ridge, there were endless halls to travel before reaching the lone exit to the middle-school grounds.

But at least here in Madison there'd be no Mickey Schrader stepping on Bo's heels and teasing him about being short. Mickey Schrader, with his freckled face and spiky-stiff red hair. Good riddance! He was the one thing about California that Bo wouldn't miss.

He paused at the edge of the blacktop and surveyed the action already taking shape. The eighth graders were getting up a game of touch football. Knots of girls dotted the grass. A couple of boys from his homeroom were flipping a Frisbee back and forth over by the bikes. Big deal.

Bo sidled along the pavement toward the elementary-school side of the playground. No one was watching, and as short as he was, it would be easy to blend in with the fifth graders out on the soccer field. At least *they* were doing something fun.

There was always tetherball. But who wanted to wait in line with a bunch of girls? Anyway, he could break his finger playing tetherball—kids at his old school were always doing that—and there would go gymnastics. . . .

Maybe he'd play scatter-dodge. But the boys were so short. Second graders, probably. One of them was sure to rat on him if he tried to bust into their game. . . .

"Hey, Bo! Wait up!"

It was Matthew. His longish, black curls were bouncing up and down like loosened springs. Bo could almost hear them making *boing-boing-boing*-ing sounds. He froze, wondering whether the greeting had attracted some teacher's attention. That's all he needed his first week of school—detention hall for going off the middle-school grounds. He'd never hear the end of it from his parents.

"Sorry I got you in trouble," Matthew said. Even hunched over, panting for breath, he was taller than Bo.

"You're the one who had to go stand in the hall."

Matthew shrugged. "Yeah, well . . . I shouldn't have laughed." He stuffed his hands in his pockets, kicking at a rock. It skittered across the blacktop and bounced off a basketball pole. "You play hockey?"

Bo shook his head. "I'm in gymnastics."

"At Capital?"

"Yeah. On the team."

"You're kidding! So's my big brother. He's thirteen. You know him? Eric Weiler?"

"Not yet," Bo said. "Practice doesn't start until Tuesday."

Matthew stood back, cocking his head. "So, are you pretty good or what?" he asked at last.

"The best." Bo grinned. This was great! He could be anything he wanted to be—even confident. "I'm going to win a gold medal."

Matthew laughed. "That's what you think. No one wins gold medals but Jim Harmon."

Bo felt like Matthew had just punched him in the stomach. "Jim Harmon? What's so special about him?"

"You'll see," Matthew said. "Just don't get your hopes up. There's no way you can beat him."

Bo scowled. What did Matthew know, anyway? Jim was probably in Eric's age group—thirteen to fifteen. Bo would never even have to compete against him. Probably.

"Whatcha doing way over here? Want to play football?" Matthew said. "Eric and his friends'll let us in."

Bo shook his head. He was thinking about the gold medal he wanted to win and this Jim Harmon guy. If he was that good, then Bo would be better. It was as simple as that. "You go on," Bo said.

"Sure?"

"Yeah. Maybe another time."

Matthew shrugged, then jogged past the duty teacher and off toward the football field. *Whew!* Bo thought. *She didn't stop Matthew, didn't see us over here on the elementary-school side.*

Edging farther from her view, Bo spied a set of chin-up bars in a sandbox beyond the blacktop. Perfect! He'd work on strength, go for a new personal best—twelve pull-ups without stopping.

Two girls were hanging upside down on the lowest bar, showing off the shorts they had worn under their skirts. Bo jumped for the middle bar but couldn't reach it. He tried again. No luck.

A knot of boys had gathered nearby. Bo felt their stares. He heard their muffled laughter, and his heart pounded faster.

"Hey, Shortie!" a tall, skinny kid called. "Need a boost?"

Bo eyed the bar above him, pressing his lips together. Who did that kid think he was, anyway? Probably nothing but a *fifth* grader. Bo'd show *him.* Shinnying up the post, he reached over and gripped the cool, smooth pipe. Then he began swinging, pumping higher and higher until his body lay straight out from the bar.

He loved the height, loved the breeze his body made as he swung to and fro. Without thinking, he did a single-leg shoot, flying upright atop the bar, his legs astride. He faced the other way, brought his back leg over, and circled forward with the bar at his hips. *Toes pointed, legs straight.* His old coach's voice rang in his head. *Now stick the dismount. . . .*

He swung up, feet atop the bar, then shot down and under it. His body arched in flight, landing perfectly feetfirst by the edge of the sandbox.

Bo was startled by a burst of applause and a few hoots behind him. They liked him! He spun about, grinning.

"What a show-off!" said the blond girl underneath the lowest bar. "Come on. Let's get out of here."

The boys were edging away, too. They were laughing and nudging each other.

Bo felt as if they'd just poured cold water on his head. He'd only set out to do pull-ups, for Pete's sake. Why did he go and do all that other stuff?

"I should've played football with Matthew," he muttered, kicking sand off his sneaker. "Next time he asks, I'll say yes. If there is a next time. . . ."

The Christopher Trap

FOR THE REST OF THE DAY, Bo could not escape the sound of kids laughing at him. They even tittered nervously when Mrs. Slater read his essay. It seemed as if they were embarrassed by what he had written. Bo could not understand why. Maybe Mom could explain their reaction . . . if she even had time to read his paper. Lately, it seemed he needed an appointment just to see her.

When he burst through the back door, the first thing he heard was the scream of a human fire engine—Christopher. After that came the distant chattering of Mom's sewing machine.

"Bo! Bo! Wanna play?" Christopher shoved a plastic fire truck into Bo's hands.

"Maybe later."

"No! Play now!" Christopher clamped his arms around Bo's leg, refusing to let go.

Bo sighed. "Come on, Chris'per. Leave me alone, will you? I want to talk to Mom."

Christopher shook his head. His bottom lip stuck out so far that Bo thought he could have tripped on it.

"Okay, okay!" Bo said. "Just get off my leg!"

Christopher let go.

Bo hung his backpack on the hook in the mudroom. Then he unzipped it and took out his windbreaker. He flicked a speck of dirt off the sleeve, then hung it in the closet. Next he fished out his lunch box and homework folder. Christopher was watching every move.

"You're not playing," he said. "I'm gonna tell Momma. You promised, Bo."

"Go tell. I don't care."

Christopher's sneakers squealed as he spun about and raced down the hall.

"A person can't even unpack his backpack, for Pete's sake," Bo muttered. "Can't even walk in the door without being nagged. . . ."

He carried the truck, his lunch box, and the folder into the kitchen and set them on the cluttered countertop. The garbage can in the corner was so full that the flapping lid would not stay down. It smelled like tuna fish. Yuck!

Bo filled a glass with milk and snapped a banana

off the bunch. The sewing machine had stopped, and he could hear Christopher pouring on the tears about how Bo had broken his promise.

Within seconds Mom burst through the swinging door from the dining room. She looked frazzled, as if she hadn't had time to comb her hair since yesterday.

"What's going on, Bo?" she asked. "I'm on a deadline here. Be a sweetie—will you?—and take Christopher off my hands for an hour or so? I've been at this all day and I haven't even gotten two orders filled!"

"I'm not surprised," Bo mumbled, his mouth full of banana.

"What was that?"

"Nothing," he said. "One hour? That's all?"

"That would be great." She ruffled his hair. "You are a love, you really are! I promise, as soon as a nursery school calls with a vacancy, things will be the way they were back home."

Back home. Bo sighed. Even Mom thought of California as home.

She called Christopher in from the dining room. "Bo's going to play with you now," she said, "and I want you to let Mommy work, okay?"

He nodded, all innocence.

Bo set his milk glass in the sink, eyeing his brother warily. Nothing seemed amiss and yet . . . Bo pushed the thought from his mind.

Mom was moving things around the cluttered countertop—his folder, his lunch box. They'd be lost by tomorrow, Bo thought as he unburied his schoolwork.

"Hey, Mom, I've got to ask you something. We had to write this essay, see? And I . . . well, wait. I want you to read it yourself."

He riffled through the papers, but couldn't find the one Mrs. Slater had awarded a big, red-inked A. "It's in here somewhere," he said.

Mom rubbed his shoulder gently. "I can see it later, can't I? Just take your time—you'll find it—and show it to me at dinner, all right?"

Bo bit his lip and nodded.

"That's my good boy. I don't know what I'd do without you, Bo." She headed toward the dining room. "See you in an hour."

Bo grabbed Christopher's hand and led him toward the stairs. He wished Mom could have waited to start up her business again until they were more settled. She still had boxes to unpack, for Pete's sake! And they were all stacked up in what was supposed to be Bo's new room. But he guessed he understood how she felt.

Back in California, it was the "in" thing to order her "Nancy's Fancies." Christopher was in preschool and Mom was so happy with all that business, she'd go around the house singing to herself. Then Dad got it in his head to join a new law firm. And now she had to start all over again. Just like Bo.

"We're going to play Candy Land, okay?"

"Only if I get gumdrop," Christopher said.

"Fine. Whatever you want."

"Oh, boy! And gingerbread, too?"

Bo sighed, trudging up beside Christopher. "Oh, okay. Gingerbread, too." For that matter he could have candy cane, lollipop, peanut brittle, the whole works. *Anything to keep him quiet,* Bo thought.

Suddenly, Mom began screeching from the dining room below. She sounded like a cat with its tail caught in a door. Christopher broke free and raced ahead to their room.

Bo let him go. He leaned over the banister, hollering down, "Mom? You okay?"

"Aaargh! Christopher cut up my material! Ruined it! Now what am I going to do?" She sounded like she was going to cry.

"Go buy more?" Bo suggested.

Mom sniffed. "I guess that's all I *can* do. I promised these smocks for tomorrow."

"I'll get Chris'per," Bo said. "He's probably hiding out."

When he tried the door to their room, it was locked. Bo rattled the knob. "Open up! You hear me?"

"Promise you won't get me?"

"Oh, for Pete's sake. I'm not going to get you like that. We're going to the store. Now open up!"

The door swung open. Bo groaned. The room was a web of blankets . . . again! One hung over the side of Christopher's top bunk. Another stretched from Bo's desktop to the windowsill. A third was draped over the chair, its corners weighted with books.

"How come you never like my fort?" Christopher asked.

Bo said nothing and ripped down the blankets.

Christopher pummeled him with his fists. "You wrecked my fort! I'm going to tell Momma!" He turned on the tears and headed downstairs.

Bo laughed. "Go tell her! That's a great idea!"

He flopped on his bed and closed his eyes. Anger pounded at his temples. If only today were Tuesday, he'd soon be heading for the gym.

The gym . . . Bo imagined it, just the way Ruiz, his old coach, had taught him. *Make it happen with the power of your mind. What you picture is what you do.* Bo smiled at the echo of Ruiz's voice. In a moment he could see himself, feel himself, on the high bar, swinging above the crowd, smiling. People were cheering, not laughing. Mom and Dad were there without Christopher. The judge was going to give him at least a nine. Maybe more. The gold medal would be his. . . .

3

Master James
Robert Harmon III

MOM ANGLED the faded-blue station wagon into a parking space in front of Capital Gymnastics Academy. "Are you sure you don't want us to come in and watch for a while?" she asked. "It *is* your first practice, after all."

Bo shook his head. "I'll be fine. Besides, Chris'per's almost asleep." Thank goodness. The last thing Bo wanted today was his brother tearing around the gym, embarrassing him. *Save that for later,* he thought. *Till I know the guys.*

"He is?" Mom turned around. She seemed surprised to see his head flopped to the side like a rag doll's. "Well, I guess he's had a hard day."

Bo grabbed his ratty, old backpack off the floor. "You'll be back at nine?"

"On the nose." Mom leaned over and kissed him. "Have a good workout."

Bo breathed the humid, late-summer evening in and waved as the car pulled out of sight.

Well, here goes, he thought, and hustled inside.

He could hear shoes thunking on the floor and guys laughing through the open doorway to his left. Poking his head around the corner, he said, "Anybody home?"

"Who wants to know?" a skinny, blond-haired boy asked. He sounded curious, not unkind.

"Bo Ragatz."

"The new hotshot from California?"

Bo grinned, plopping his backpack on a bench. "That what they told you?"

"Yep." The blond kid pulled his gym slippers on, said his name was Jed Lewis.

He introduced the other guys, but Jim Harmon was not among them. Everyone was taller than Bo except for a kid named Denny—and *he* was a fourth grader. What could you expect?

"Come on," Jed said. "I'll show you around."

Bo changed quickly. He and Jed were heading toward the main gym when someone yelled, "Hey, Ragatz, wanna see a grand entrance, Harmonstyle?"

"Harmon?" Bo's pulse quickened. "You mean like in Jim Harmon?"

Jed nodded and hustled Bo back through the dressing room and into the hall. The all-glass front door revealed a long, silver car pulling to a stop in front of the building. Its front grille resembled the side of a stainless-steel bird cage. A statuette of a lady in flowing robes was perched on the hood.

"It's a Rolls," Jed said. "Is that amazing or what?"

"Amazing," Bo breathed. "The guy must be loaded!"

"You mean you don't know him? I thought you lived in the Bluff."

Bo shook his head. "Eric Weiler's brother's in my class. He says nobody beats Jim. Is that right?"

Jed shrugged. "Check this," he said, nudging Bo.

A man had gotten out of the Rolls and was walking around to open the back door. He wore slacks, a polo shirt, and an expression of boredom as he helped Jim from the backseat.

"Is that his dad?" Bo asked.

"Are you kidding?" Jed laughed. "His old man only blows into town when we've got a meet. He's too busy traveling around, selling hockey sticks or something. That guy's Jim's driver."

Bo slapped his own cheek and teased, "Well, pardon me."

"Make way for King James," muttered the tallest boy in the group. He grunted in disgust and stalked off.

"What's with him?" Bo whispered.

"Phil?" Jed shrugged. "Just jealous, I guess."

The boy who jumped out of the Rolls was tall and

tan. He had wavy, blond hair that was partly plastered down. The rest was starting to frizz. A fancy, red-and-blue gym bag was slung over his shoulder. It was just like the one in the window of Sampson's that Bo had been begging Mom for last week.

Jim approached the building with a springy, confident walk, and his head seemed to grow two sizes when he saw the cluster of boys in the hall.

One of the guys made a phony trumpet sound and announced, "Now arriving, Master James Robert Harmon the Third."

"That's my name," Jim said. "Don't wear it out. What's all this? Don't tell me. Let me guess. You guys missed me!" He scanned the crowd. His eyes were the color of nails, steely gray. They narrowed at Bo. "Who are you? The new Wonder Boy?"

"If you say so." Bo smiled to show that he was only teasing.

But Jim elbowed past. "We'll just see about that, Shrimpboat," he said, and disappeared into the dressing room.

Shrimpboat, was it? Bo glared in Jim's direction, pursing his lips. That was even worse than Mickey Schrader calling him Shortcake! Every nasty word Bo had ever heard surged through his mind. Only *jerk* slipped out.

"Aw, don't let him get to you," Jed said. "He's okay. Sort of. You just got to know how to take him."

"You mean it's not just me?"

Jed shook his head. "I doubt it."

Bo frowned. "Then what?"

"Your scores, probably. Coach sent out a news-letter and gave you some buildup."

"Oh, yeah. That." Bo remembered how proud he'd felt, reading his new coach's welcome in the team bulletin, and how he'd hurried to paste it into his scrapbook.

"Just forget him," Jed said. "Come on. Let's go warm up."

Bo nodded. He'd waited weeks for this first prac-tice and wasn't about to let anything spoil it. Espe-cially not Jim Harmon! One thing at least was a relief. The guy had to be at least thirteen, too old to com-pete in Bo's age group.

The high-ceilinged gym seemed smaller than Bo's old one in California. Maybe, he thought, it was just the lack of mirrors. The trampoline and foam-filled practice pit looked different, too. Neither was sunk into the floor, but Bo supposed that wouldn't matter. Everything else was the same—a large, square, spring floor in the center surrounded by rings, pommel and vaulting horses, a high bar, and a set of parallel bars.

Bo breathed the familiar smell of chalk dust and smiled. Already the place felt like home. Pulling his sweatpants' drawstring tighter, he approached the man with the clipboard.

"You the coach?"

The man looked up and nodded. He had the face of an overgrown kid and an eager grin that set Bo at ease. "Jack Sweeney. Call me Jack. You must be Bo. I must say, we've heard mighty good things about you."

Bo stood up taller.

"You sure got lucky, training with Eli Ruiz, you know that?"

Bo nodded, and Jack continued, "Darn shame the way that knee injury knocked him out of the Olympics. I was still in high school when it happened. But heck, I felt like I knew the guy after watching him wipe out on national TV." Jack shook his head. "Poor old Eli. He was our best hope that year against the Russians, too."

Bo pressed his lips together and said nothing. He'd known about Ruiz's injury—news stories about his old coach's entire career were plastered all over the gym back home—but the guy was so up about everything, Bo had never thought to feel sorry for him.

"Well," Jack said, marking something on his clipboard, "are you looking forward to competing this year?"

"Sure am!" Bo brightened. "I thought my practice-team year would never be over."

"Ruiz never let you compete?"

Bo shook his head.

"Then where did he get those scores he sent me? Those fifties and fifty-ones?"

"He gave me those in practice," Bo said.

"Oh, he did, did he?" Jack stepped back. His expression changed from sunny to cloudy-with-a-chance-of-rain. "Well, go on. Warm up. Then we'll see what you can do."

Goose bumps were popping up all over Bo's arms as he sat down to stretch. *Maybe I'm not good enough,* he thought. *Maybe Jack won't even let me be on the team!*

4

Chalk Dust Flies

BO SNEAKED a look at Jim, who was off by himself, sitting in a wide straddle. Jim's whole body lay flat on the mat. The guy was as flexible as Silly Putty.

Bo tried to copy the position, but he knew his stomach was still at least a hand's width off the floor. He pounded his fists on his thighs, but they would not give way.

Other boys wandered in until there were about a dozen scattered across the floor. At the end of warm-ups another coach came in, a college guy named Stu, and announced the boys in each practice squad.

"Jed Lewis, Phil Bender, Denny Spencer, Eric Weiler, Jim Harmon, and Bo Ragatz—you guys are with Jack this week. The rest of you are with me."

A couple of guys groaned.

"You don't like it," Stu said with a mischievous

24

smirk, "you can always do push-ups for three hours."

Bo jumped to his feet and joined Jack's squad beneath the rings.

"Okay, chalk up, everybody," Jack said. "Let's see how rusty you've all gotten."

Bo joined Jed at the chalk bucket and dusted his hands lightly. He noticed Jim run back to the dressing room.

"Where's he going?" Bo asked.

Jed shrugged.

Jim returned moments later, clutching a pair of leather grips. He made a big show of wriggling his fingers into the holes and wrapping the Velcro straps around his wrists. Then he chalked up.

Bo looked at his own white, callused palms. "What's all that?" he whispered to Jed.

"His lucky grips."

"You're kidding me."

"That's what *he* calls them," Jed said. "See for yourself."

Jack lifted Jim up to the rings and stepped aside.

Jim swung up to an inverted hang, his body like an arrow. Then he completed two inlocates—full forward circles from a hanging position—and didn't even pike! His body was absolutely straight as he swung through the inverted position!

Slowly he lowered his legs into an L-hang. They were perfectly parallel with the floor. His stomach muscles tensed as he held the position. Then he swung backward and forward into another inverted hang, and piked into his dislocate—a move that looked as if his shoulders did exactly that.

Two more swings and Jim sailed up into his tuck flyaway dismount with such grace and precision that Bo could hardly breathe. He stuck his landing without even a hop. The guy was brilliant!

"Wow! That was great!" Bo said.

"What did you expect?" Jim clapped his leather-covered hands together and coughed at the chalk dust. "These babies never let me down."

"But it was you who—"

Jack silenced Bo with a snap of his fingers. "Ragatz, go! Show us your stuff."

Bo gulped. He stepped onto the thick mat and looked up at the rings. They were a long way up. Panic rushed through him. He could never match Jim's style. He'd be doing great to nail his landing. Maybe Jack wouldn't even want him. . . .

"Come on, Ragatz. Don't be shy," Jack said.

Bo felt Jack's hands around his waist. He reached for the rings and jumped as Jack lifted. The familiar feel of smooth wood in his hands edged aside his fears.

Faces blurred below as Bo pumped higher and higher. In his inverted hang, he remembered to keep his head in neutral and not to arch his back. So far, so good.

His inlocates flowed smoothly enough, but they weren't straight body like Jim's. Still, his legs were taut, his toes pointed. *I'll wow them with great form, if nothing else,* he thought.

He didn't get hung up on his dislocate, and he could sense he'd gotten good height on his tuck flyaway. *Now to stick it!* He spotted the ground, bent his knees, and connected solidly with the mat. His arms spread upward in a triumphant V.

Jack tucked his clipboard under his arm and started to clap. The other boys joined in. They crowded around Bo, slapping hands and congratu-lating him. Bo soaked up their praise.

"Hey, Harmon," Phil Bender said, "it's about time you had a little competition."

It was then that Bo realized Jim Harmon was not among his admirers. He was standing over by the wall, his arms folded across his chest. His eyes brimmed with anger.

"W-what do you mean, competition?" Bo said, looking from Phil to Jim and back again. "He's in thirteen-to-fifteens, isn't he?"

"Doesn't he wish," Phil said. "When do you turn thirteen, Harmon? Not soon enough, I'll bet."

Jim stuck out his chin. His eyes looked all watery.

Bo's mouth hung open. He couldn't seem to close it. Jim Harmon was still twelve and in Bo's age group? He was so tall . . . talked so tough. It seemed impossible that he wasn't older.

"All right, Bender," Jack cut in, "lay off him, will you? In fact, why don't you go work out with Stu? He's got mostly older guys tonight anyway. Send Myers over here."

Phil muttered something and jogged toward the vault.

The guy who took his place, Tony Myers, was eleven, maybe twelve. But he had one of those soldier-boy haircuts that made his face look old. Tony headed for Jim like a moth to a spotlight.

"Hey, Jim, be cool," he said, and punched Jim's arm playfully.

Jim brushed a chalky, grip-covered hand over Tony's stubbly hair. "Buzz off, Buzzhead!" he said.

Tony made his eyes bug out and his cheeks bulge in response. Jim glared at the newcomer's fish face, but soon his lips edged upward, and Bo could see the anger fading from Jim's eyes.

"Now I have to wash my hair," Tony joked in a put-on girl's voice.

"All right, you two. Settle down or I'll sit you out for a while," Jack said. "Weiler, you're up."

Bo stepped off the mat so Eric could take his turn. He stole another glance at Jim and his sidekick, Tony. They stood apart from everyone. *Like it's them against us,* Bo thought. *Why are they choosing sides? This is supposed to be a team, not a battlefield!*

He plopped down dejectedly. Things weren't like this in California, that was for sure. There, the guys actually helped each other. What mattered was the team. That, and making progress. "A *judge* doesn't make you a winner," Ruiz used to say. "*You* do, just by beating your personal best."

What this team needed was a pep talk, Bo thought. But right now that seemed the farthest thing from Jack's mind as he pushed the other boys through their paces on the rings.

Bo tried to take his mind off Jim by watching their routines. Eric kept getting hung up on the dislocate. Jed needed work on his form. Denny Spencer was obviously the youngest kid on the team and it showed. He couldn't even swing without piking at the waist. Tony, on the other hand, was so double-jointed that he bent practically in half on the back-swing.

It was easy to see now what Phil meant about giving Jim some competition. And it was easy to see why Eric had told his brother that Jim Harmon couldn't be beat. But if anyone could, it was Bo Ragatz. Of that much, he was sure.

Just the thought made Bo brave Jim's icy stare with a grin.

5

A Real Stumper

BO HUNCHED over the kitchen table, thinking about his math assignment. He was supposed to write a word problem, a real stumper.

Tomorrow, Friday, all the kids would turn them in for Mrs. Slater to ditto off. Sometime next week they'd have a crack at each other's problems. The one who solved the most would be named to the middle school's math team.

How about this? he asked himself, and began to write: "Bo has spent six hours a week for four weeks with Jim. How many hours have they hated each other?"

He crossed out that last part and rewrote it: "How many hours have they *known* each other?"

"Let's see . . . ," Bo said aloud, then multiplied

six times four. "Twenty-four hours? That's a whole day and night!"

He couldn't believe it. It felt like a lot longer, and yet he hardly knew Jim Harmon at all.

Obviously, the guy was rich (anybody driven around in a Rolls Royce had to be), and his mom and dad were too busy to show their faces at the gym. Some of the guys hated him, most put up with him, and a couple even seemed to like him. But it was clear that Jim Harmon saved his worst side for Bo.

And though he tried to ignore Jim, like Jed said, it wasn't easy. Even Mom called Jim a spoiled brat, and it wasn't like her to judge anybody.

Bo reread his math problem and decided to make it trickier. He changed the last part to "How many *days* have they known each other?" Everyone would answer in hours. He was sure of it. Or else they'd say twenty-eight days—the four weeks times seven days. And they'd all be wrong!

The twist so delighted him that he copied it over in his best cursive, humming the "Jeopardy" theme song softly to himself.

When he glanced at the wall clock, it was already four-thirty. He still had to do his spelling sentences and history questions before gym practice. At least Christopher was upstairs, helping Mom fold laundry all over Mom and Dad's bed. It sure beat having him interrupt every five seconds with another burning question.

As Bo flipped to Spelling Lesson Five, the back door opened and slammed shut. By the clomp of the footsteps, Bo knew it was Dad. He bolted out of his chair and down the hall.

Dad held out both hands as if to stop traffic. His forehead was all scrunched up into little lines.

"Dad! Hi! You want to see my math stumper?"

"Sure do, Bozer," he said. "But could I just grab a couple of aspirin? Maybe even lie down for a bit? I've got a killer of a headache."

"It's okay with me," Bo said, "but Mom's got clothes all over the bed."

"Great," Dad said glumly. He loosened his tie and started up the stairs, calling back over his shoulder, "You finish up your homework now, hear me? Otherwise, no gymnastics."

Bo did not reply. What did Dad think Bo was doing, anyway? Making up story problems for fun?

"Bo?" came his father's voice. "I'm not kidding around. If your grades start slipping, you're off the team. Understand?"

"Yes, sir," Bo shot back. He held his breath. Had Dad found something disrespectful in his tone? Bo didn't want to get him angry. After all, Dad could make him stay home from practice tonight . . . or maybe even miss the minimeet against Salto on Sunday!

That's the thing about dads, Bo thought. *They're like puppet masters, always pulling your strings.* One jerk and you could end up moving halfway across the country—to a place like *Wisconsin,* with air so thick you can't even breathe and stinky hog farms and a creep named Jim Harmon.

Dad must have been satisfied, because the next thing Bo heard was him shooing Mom and Christopher out of the bedroom. "And Nance," Dad called after her, "keep the kids quiet, will you? I have to shake this headache! I've got a client coming over tonight."

"I'll try," Mom said. But Bo could hear the edge in her voice, and she closed the door harder than she had to.

Bo busied himself with spelling as she dragged a kicking, screaming Christopher up the hall toward the kitchen.

"I wanna see Daddy! Lemme go!"

"Shhhh! Christopher, be quiet!" Mom hissed. "Dad's trying to sleep!" She eyed the ceiling with something like dread. "Come on. Let's all play that game you like. Pirate Treasure? Treasure Quest?"

"You mean, Lost Treasure?" Bo said.

Christopher went limp and mute in the same moment. His eyes brightened.

"Okay, boys?" Mom looked from one to the other. "First one to a million dollars wins."

Bo sighed. "I've got all this homework. And Dad won't let me go to gym if I don't—"

"One little game," she begged, adding in a whisper, "We can cheat and let Christopher win, okay?"

"Please, Bo," his brother wheedled. "I like doing the air-tank thing."

Bo sighed and glanced up at the clock. He still had time. "Oh, all right," he said. "As long as we make it quick."

He cleared the kitchen table off while Mom and Christopher set up the game board with three colored pirate ships. The phone rang and Mom leaped to answer it.

Bo passed out the money, ignoring the interruption. After Mom hung up, she sank into the chair beside Bo. An apology was written all over her face.

"Now what?" Bo said.

"You're never going to believe it. That was Rock-A-Bye. Mrs. Lester's order is missing. She called to check and it wasn't in with the stuff I delivered today." Mom shook her head. "I just can't understand it because I remember doing the 'Melanie' appliqué."

"Maybe you're going crazy," Bo suggested.

"Maybe I am."

Bo looked accusingly at Christopher but said nothing. "What are you going to do?" he asked.

"I've got to sew a new one. Mrs. Gentry said if it's not there before they close tonight, I can kiss this account good-bye." She eyed the game board guiltily. "What can I do, Bo? I'm sorry."

"I didn't want to play anyway, remember? I've still got homework."

Christopher's face was all drawn up, ready to cry.

"Please, Christopher," Mom said, "try to understand."

"He'll get over it."

"I know but . . ." Mom's voice trailed off. She looked like she was fighting a war inside her head. "It's not fair of me to ask you this, Bo, I know, but . . ."

"I'll watch him," Bo said, "if you buy me that gym bag at Sampson's."

"No bribes." But her expression softened. "Well, I'll think about it."

"Okay," Bo said. A *maybe* was better than nothing. "Go sew your apron thing."

"Smock," Mom corrected.

"Whatever."

Mom smooched his forehead with a big, wet kiss that Bo couldn't wait to wipe off. "We'll have pineapple burgers for supper," she promised. "The meat's just about defrosted."

"Goody!" Bo conjured up the tangy ketchup-mustard-and-brown-sugar smell of the sauce that accompanied his favorite burgers. "Can you hurry? Please?" he said, then added, "I'm starving," to mask his frustration at having to watch Christopher again.

Mom scooted through the kitchen. The dining-room door flapped to and fro behind her, then finally fell silent.

Bo turned to Christopher, who was now poking numbers on the Lost Treasure computer. "I'll make you a deal," he offered. "You can stay here and hunt for treasure, and I'll go in the den and finish my homework, okay?"

Christopher shook his head. "You play, too. You do the numbers so I can dive."

Bo sighed. "Look, Chris'per. That's a really boring way to play. I'm saying you can push the numbers *and* dive, don't you see?"

Christopher grinned broadly. He looked kind of cute, Bo thought, even with those little buckteeth. "I can do everything? All by myself?"

Bo nodded quickly.

"Well . . . okay."

Bo swept his books off the kitchen counter before Christopher could change his mind. He retreated to the den and tried to ignore the *zap, zap, zap* of Christopher pushing the wrong buttons. He was hunkered over Dad's rolltop desk, halfway through his spelling, when Christopher started whining.

"It's broken, Bo. I can't find the treasure and I wanna dive!"

"Try again," Bo called absently.

Zap, zap, zap. "Do it for me, Bo!"

"In a minute," he said. "I'm almost done."

Much more than a minute had passed, Bo realized, when something caught his attention. A distant *thwack, thwack* sound. He stopped writing and stared straight ahead, seeing nothing. There it was again! It seemed to be coming from the kitchen.

Raining Hamburger

"CHRIS'PER?" Bo called. "What are you doing?"

"Nothing. Just playing."

In a moment, Bo heard it again. *Thwack, thwack.* Slapping his speller on the desk, he stormed off to check on his brother.

When he reached the kitchen, he found Christopher sitting on the floor, surrounded by clumps of hamburger. His brother giggled like a hyena.

Bo did not see anything funny. "Pick up that hamburger!" he hissed. "You're gonna get us both in trouble!"

"Look, Bo! It's raining hamburger." Christopher collapsed onto his back, still laughing, and pointed at the ceiling.

Bo gulped, afraid to follow his brother's finger. When he finally looked up, he could only gasp.

37

Smeared all over the white ceiling were huge, reddish globs. They looked like blood and guts. Or at least, the way Bo imagined blood and guts would look. Mom and Dad were going to cancel gymnastics for sure when they saw that!

Bo glared at Christopher. "You just sit there," he ordered. "Don't you dare move! And keep quiet!"

Christopher dragged himself off the floor, his eyes suddenly wide. It was as if he had just that moment seen the terrible thing he had done.

Bo rolled a chair into the center of the kitchen, piled the phone book on top, and grabbed a wet, soapy sponge. He clambered up, ready to take a swipe at the mess, but he was still too short.

"What made you do such a stupid thing?" Bo demanded. "I can't even believe it. And who's going to get in trouble? Me!"

Christopher's bottom lip quivered. He looked like a cornered rabbit. Bo almost felt sorry for him. Almost, but not quite.

"Just stay there," Bo said. "I'm getting more books."

He returned with some heavy law tomes from the den and stacked them on top of the phone book.

"Hold the chair, Chris'per."

Christopher's knuckles went white as he grabbed onto the high, vinyl-covered back with both hands.

Bo rewet the sponge and climbed up.

The awful mess loomed before him now, almost within reach. Maybe if he just went on tiptoe . . .

Bo rose onto his toes, sweeping the sponge in a wide, futile arc across the ceiling. As he did, he felt his balance change, felt the chair move. He was falling, falling, an instant played out in slow motion.

He heard the sharp intake of his breath.

He felt his temple smack against the cold, metal chair leg.

The thud of his body hitting the floor kept echoing as if in a bad dream. Echoing . . . echoing . . . Growing softer and softer . . . until there was nothing.

The next thing Bo saw was a blur of hovering faces. He struggled to sit up, but a firm hand eased him back to the floor. With great effort, he focused his eyes.

"Just relax now. That's right. You're going to be fine," Dad said. " 'Atta boy."

Mom had the portable telephone clapped to her ear. Someone—Christopher?—was pressing a wet cloth against Bo's forehead.

"I'm okay," Bo said. "Just let me finish my homework so I can go to gymnastics."

"Whoa, Bozer. You're not going anywhere. Not till we let the doctor take a look at that gash."

Bo touched the cloth. It felt sticky. When he looked at his fingers, they were smeared with red. He swallowed hard, allowing himself to feel the dull, throbbing pain. Something churned deep in his gut. His throat closed off and he began to sweat.

"I think . . . I'm gonna . . . be sick."

As he started to cough, Dad rolled him onto his side.

"It's okay," Dad whispered. "Don't worry about the floor."

Bo retched at Christopher's feet.

Christopher jumped back, screaming, "Gross! Gross!"

Bo grimaced at the foul taste.

Dad offered him a wet washrag to suck on.

Bo smiled weakly. He watched Mom hang up the phone. Her face looked as pale as the almost-white countertops.

"Dr. Bollen says we should get him to the hospital," she reported. "He'll meet us there."

"Maybe I'd better carry him," Dad said. "You get Chris."

Dad scooped Bo into his arms.

He felt like a dumb baby, being cradled like that. But something made him reach one arm up and wrap it around Dad's neck. That same something made him start to cry.

"It's okay, Bozer. You'll see."

Bo sniffed. "I'm sorry I messed up, Dad."

"You didn't mess up."

"I should have been watching Christopher," Bo

said, "but I was doing my homework. I should have—"

"You should have been doing your homework," Dad said gently. "Chris is your mom's responsibility, not yours."

Bo couldn't see Mom's face. She was looking at the floor. Or maybe down at Christopher.

"I had an order to fill," she said evenly. "Either that or lose the whole Rock-A-Bye account. Who would have thought . . ." Her voice trailed off. She shook her head.

"What about your smock?" Bo said.

Mom shrugged. "I'll worry about that later. Right now, I'm much more concerned about you."

Bo touched the cloth and winced. He'd messed things up all right. Mom's order. His homework. Dad's nap. Even Dad's meeting with that business guy. And, of course, gymnastics. There was no way he could go to practice tonight. And what about Sunday?

"I *will* be able to go to the minimeet, won't I?" he said.

Bo looked from Dad to Mom. Neither one answered. They eyed each other, then the floor.

Gym Bags

THE WORST THING about Bo's mild concussion and four stitches was the pain of not being able to compete in the minimeet. Mom and Dad wouldn't even let him go to watch.

The best thing was Mom finally agreeing to buy him the red-and-blue gym bag from Sampson's.

By Tuesday afternoon the window of the mall's large sporting-goods store was filled with stuffed Bucky Badgers, red-and-white Wisconsin football jerseys, and soccer balls and cleats. The gym bag, however, was nowhere in sight.

"I bet it's gone." Bo sighed.

"Now, now. Don't give up," Mom said. "Let's ask someone."

She and Bo approached the sales desk. Christopher tagged behind.

The clerk had his back to them. He and another man, a big, silver-haired guy wearing a thick, gold chain around his neck, were talking behind the counter.

"What can I say to change your mind?" the gold-chain guy was saying. "You saw what's happened since the '84 Olympics. Gymnastics is the up-and-coming sport. Mark my words. Nowhere else in town carries shoes or grips or uniforms even. The poor kids have to order them out, then wait a year and a Christmas for the stuff to come in. And what happens? Nothing fits."

The mention of gymnastics caught Bo's attention and he drew closer.

"I don't know," the salesclerk said. "How many kids are we talking? Ten, fifteen, tops? We'll have to think about it."

"Be my guest. Meantime my son will be raking in the gold medals. Maybe you could use him in an ad campaign."

"He's that good, huh?" The clerk sounded interested.

"A born winner. He knows better than to bring home second place, know what I mean?" The big guy winked.

Bo wondered about his son, about what class he competed in. Surely he wasn't a beginning Class IV like Bo. He was probably on the university team. Either that or he competed in high school.

He *had* to because his father looked way older than Dad.

"I can't believe his attitude," Mom whispered to Bo. "I feel sorry for his son." She edged closer, cleared her throat.

The salesclerk held up a finger. "Be right with you, ma'am," he said.

The big guy assembled some papers and put them in a leather briefcase. "You let me know what you think, okay? I'll be coming through town in a couple of weeks. Maybe we can do lunch."

Coming through town. A crazy thought flitted through Bo's mind. Maybe the guy was *Jim's* father! Hadn't Jed said he traveled around, selling hockey stuff or something like that? Maybe he sold other sporting goods, too. And the kid he was bragging about was Jim! No, Bo thought. The guy looked too old to have a twelve-year-old son.

Mom tapped the man's arm as he strode around the counter. "Excuse me," she said. "This is none of my business, I know, but . . ."

Bo cringed. He couldn't believe she was telling a total stranger that winning wasn't everything!

The man blinked patiently, waiting for her to finish. "Perhaps if your son was in competition," he said, "you'd feel differently."

"My son *is* in competition—"

"Well, perhaps if he showed real talent."

Color rose in Mom's cheeks. Bo's own felt warm, too. He tugged at her hand, but she didn't budge.

"He's *very* talented," Mom said. "And he competes for the joy of it."

Bo rolled his eyes. How could she be so dumb? Didn't she know all he cared about was winning, just like the man's son?

He slunk off in search of Christopher and found him hiding in the middle of a circular rack of jogging suits.

"Come on," Bo said. "Let's find that gym bag so we can get out of here."

"I'll find it!" Christopher said. He tore down one aisle after another. Bo chased after him. They found the bag in the back corner on special clearance.

"Good work, Chris'per."

Bo toted the bag to the checkout counter. He was relieved to see the gold-chain guy heading for the front door.

"Dumb jock," Mom muttered. She brightened at the sight of the gym bag. "Oh, good. I'm glad you found it."

"Yeah," he said. "Me, too." He glanced at Mom's watch. Even with it upside down he could tell that gym practice hadn't started yet. "As long as we're out," he said casually, "maybe we could stop by Capital."

Mom tweaked his chin. "I suppose you think

you're well enough to practice? You haven't even been back to school yet."

"I know. But I'd be real careful. Wouldn't even go upside down if you didn't want me to."

"I don't know. I think you're pushing things."

"Oh, please? Please, can I?"

"May I," Mom corrected.

"Whatever. You know what I mean." Bo put on a sad puppy face, but Mom wasn't even looking. She was dragging Christopher out of his jogging-suit hideaway.

"Oh, all right," she said at last. "But I don't want you doing those twirly things on the rings."

"Inlocates," Bo supplied.

"Whatever." Mom's smile mirrored his own.

On the way to the car, her good mood faded. Bo wondered out loud whether she was having second thoughts about practice. Mom shook her head.

"Then what's wrong?" he asked.

"That man," she said. "That . . . that *father*. Parents like him give sports a bad name. All that pressure to win. As if that's what it's all about."

"Mo-om!" Bo hugged his new gym bag to his chest. "Of course that's what it's all about! Why do it," he said, "if you don't want to win? What's the point?"

"The point is to have fun. To keep improving and be proud of your progress. If you happen to win, great! But a gold medal's not going to bring you happiness. Not really."

Bo rolled his eyes. "Oh, Mom!" What did she know? He bet she'd never won a gold medal in her life.

Mom shook her head, unlocked the passenger door, and held it open. "I don't get it, Bo. You never had this thing about winning last year."

"That's because I couldn't compete last year. It was just practice, don't you see?" Bo hopped in and buckled up.

"I don't know." Mom stared at his window as if an answer were written there. "Maybe I should have a little talk with your new coach." She slammed his door, settled Christopher into the backseat, and climbed in at last, firing up the station wagon.

"It's not Jack. Please," Bo blurted, "just leave it alone, will you?"

The growl of the engine seemed to nag Mom for a decision. "Okay," she sighed, "but you'd better make sure you keep your priorities straight, young man, understand?"

"I understand."

Within ten minutes he was at Capital, his new gym bag slung over his shoulder. He burst into the changing room, eager to hear about the minimeet, but froze when he saw that Jim Harmon was the only guy there.

Jim's back was toward Bo, who approached hesitantly.

"Hi," Bo said.

Jim poked his head through his T-shirt. Most of his blond waves were gone and the back of his neck was pink and itchy looking. When he turned around, he seemed annoyed.

"Oh, it's you." Jim eyed Bo's gym bag. "What a copycatter!"

"I am not." Bo scowled. "I wanted this one way before I ever even saw yours."

"Sure you did," Jim said. He turned his back toward Bo again and wriggled into a pair of white gym shorts. "What do I care? I've got a new one."

"So what."

"So aren't you going to get one just like it?" Jim spun about, waving a black-and-gold Nike bag in Bo's face. "Check it out real good. You can get 'em at Wes Zulty's."

"I like this one," Bo said quietly.

"I'll bet." Jim dropped his new bag on the floor and kicked it under the bench. "Anyway, how come you weren't at the meet?"

"You really want to know?"

Jim nodded.

Bo pulled his hair back to show off his stitches.

Jim said, "That doesn't look so bad."

Bo pressed his lips together. "Yeah, well, I had a concussion, too."

"Sure you did!" Jim laughed. "I'll bet you were just chicken—scared of getting beat."

"Was not," Bo said, stepping closer. His eyes stared right at the T.S.S. FAIRSKY on Jim's T-shirt.

Jim put his hand on Bo's head and measured. Bo came right to the middle of Jim's neck. "How old are you again, Shrimpboat? Nine?"

Bo wanted to rip the smirk right off Jim's face. Instead he jerked away. "Why don't you just leave me alone?" he said. "What did I ever do to you?"

Jim said nothing. He leaned over and started fishing through his new gym bag. Bo watched with interest from the other side of the small room as he pulled on his sweatpants.

"Quit staring! Haven't you ever seen Tiger gym shoes before?" Jim said. He slipped them on.

Bo shook his head. Why should he care about Jim's dumb old shoes?

"I bet your dad can't get *you* all the newest sports stuff," Jim said. "Mine can get stuff that isn't even in the stores yet."

Bo thought about the gold-chain guy at Sampson's. Maybe he *was* Jim's father after all. So what if he did give him all the latest sports stuff? Big deal. It didn't sound like he was home long enough to even play catch. No matter how busy Dad was, Bo could usually count on him to squeeze in a quick game. "So?" Bo said. "So what if your dad buys you the Statue of Liberty. What does that prove?"

Jim pulled out his lucky grips and dangled them in front of Bo's face. "Proves you're jealous, that's what. Proves you're never going to beat me, so you may as well stop trying."

Bo sighed. "You know, this is really stupid. We *are* on the same team, for Pete's sake."

Jim shook his head. "You're so weird, Ragatz. Short . . . and weird."

"Yeah? And what about you—you . . . Jim Bags!" Bo's face flushed as he spat out the first thing that popped into his mind. Jim Bags. How dumb could he get?

Jim slapped his grips menacingly against his hand. "Say that again, Shrimpboat, and I'll—"

"Jim Bags! Jim Bags!"

Bo danced around the room, singing out the stupid name. Suddenly, someone grabbed his shoulder from behind and spun him about.

Double Trouble

THE COACH'S ANGER filled the room like a thunder cloud. Even Jack's thick, dark hair seemed to bristle with rage. "What in the world is going on in here?" he roared. "I could hear you all the way upstairs!"

"N-nothing," Bo said.

"Don't tell me 'nothing,' Ragatz! We never had any trouble around here until . . ." Jack broke off. "Look. We've all got to pull together, okay?"

"That's just what I was telling Bo," Jim said.

Bo gritted his teeth and eyed the floor.

"All right now," Jack said. "I don't want to have any more trouble. You got it?"

Bo nodded without looking up. He blinked back the tears that came without warning.

"Come on, come on," Jack said, rubbing Bo's back. "Let's not let this ruin practice."

Bo shook his head but said nothing. Part of him wanted to call Mom and tell her he wasn't feeling as well as he'd thought. The other part wanted to go out there and show Jim Harmon that Bo Ragatz was here to stay.

"You go on," Bo said at last. "I'm going to wash up first."

The guys were still warming up when he returned. Bo sat down between Eric and Tony and began stretching out. Jack towered over them, making notes on his clipboard. At last he cleared his throat.

"Okay, guys, listen up," he said. "I'm gonna say this once, and I want you to get it and get it good. It takes more than one guy to make a team. We need all of you, pulling together, not tearing each other down. Every one of you is a winner in my book because you're out there trying. So don't let me hear any more bickering or name-calling, you guys got it?"

Jim grinned smugly as if he'd told Jack what to say. Bo's cheeks flushed. Tony Myers was staring at him. So were a couple of the older guys, Pete Carboni and Dave Payton.

"I'm talking to all of you," Jack said. "You got it?"

Bo and the others nodded.

"Okay, let's get to work. Our first big meet's right around the corner," Jack reminded them.

For the rest of the evening, Bo avoided Jim and all the twirly things, just as he'd promised Mom. It would never do to have her angry at him, too. Besides, Bo could tell from the few tricks he threw that he wasn't quite back to normal.

"Give it a couple weeks," Jack advised. "You ought to be tip-top for the Red Gym meet."

I ought to be, Bo thought, *as long as I steer clear of Jim and keep my grades up.* When he put it like that, it almost sounded easy. . . .

Bo kept telling himself that the next day at school when Mrs. Slater handed him a list of everything he'd missed. He skimmed the paper for the math-team qualifier. It wasn't there.

"You didn't do the story problems yet?" he asked.

Mrs. Slater shook her head. "With you gone and Jenny out with the flu, well, it didn't seem quite fair. I thought we'd do them first thing this morning."

"Great! What should I do with my problem?"

Mrs. Slater frowned. "I've already put everyone else's on a ditto. Let's see. Why don't you just write it on the board?"

Bo nodded and went to his desk to get the problem. He waved at Matthew, who was doodling a Lamborghini on his desktop. It wasn't bad, either. But Bo knew Mrs. Slater would make Matthew scrub desktops for a week if she saw it.

Bo sat down, opened his desk, and hid behind the lid.

"Psst! Matthew!"

Matthew grinned and started to lift his lid, too.

"No!" Bo made a frantic, downward gesture, then pointed toward Mrs. Slater. "The car!"

Matthew nodded and closed his desk. He laid his hand over the drawing, but couldn't quite hide the sports car's back end.

Bo grabbed his math problem off a pile of neatly stacked papers and stopped beside Matthew's desk.

"Are you all better?" Matthew whispered.

Bo nodded, his eyes trained on Mrs. Slater. She had been handing out the dittoed math stumpers to the first person in each row. But now she was heading their way.

Casually, Bo set his paper on Matthew's desk, covering the rest of the Lamborghini. Matthew's eyes darted from his desk to Mrs. Slater and back again. Bo held his breath. Maybe she was headed for the water fountain in the back of the room. Then again, maybe she wasn't.

"Do you two have a problem here?" she asked.

Matthew just sat there, blinking.

Bo struggled for words. "I-I was just asking Matthew if he would write my math problem up on the board for me," he said.

"Why can't you do it?" Mrs. Slater asked.

"Well, I can, of course. But, well, Matt's a lot taller and, you know, he could write it up high so everyone could see."

"Oh." She nodded as if that were the most logical explanation in the world. "Well, go ahead."

She returned to her desk.

Matthew beamed his gratitude at Bo. Then he took the paper to the board and copied Bo's problem so high even an ant sitting behind Bo could have seen it.

Bo, meanwhile, licked his fingers and smudged away all traces of the car before returning to his seat. Everyone else seemed to have a copy of the math problems. Bo was about to raise his hand and ask for one when he noticed the girl in front of him, sitting there, sniffing ditto fumes off his. He tapped her shoulder.

"Oh, sorry, Bo." She giggled and flashed him a smile. "I just love that smell, don't you?"

Bo shrugged.

"Too bad about your accident. It was my idea to make you that humongous card. Did you like it?"

Bo nodded. "It was great. Thanks."

"Too bad about your gym meet."

"Yeah," Bo said, "I know." He held out his hand for the work sheet. She stole one last whiff, giggled again, and finally handed it over. As she spun about, her long, blond pigtail swished across his desk. The paper sailed to the floor.

Bo craned his neck to see whether Mrs. Slater was looking. She was. And though she said nothing, her eyes spoke for her.

He scurried after the paper, then slumped into his chair, resting his chin on the desk. Out of the corner of his eye, he saw Matthew do the same.

Bo clapped his hand over his mouth to contain the laughter that bubbled up like soda fizz. His cheeks bulged with the effort.

Don't even look at the guy, he told himself. *Stay out of trouble.*

At last the fit passed, and Bo drew a deep but hesitant breath. Everything was fine. . . and probably would be, as long as he kept his eyes off Matthew.

"Now," Mrs. Slater said, "if you all have a copy, we'll begin. Don't forget to do Bo's problem, and remember, anybody who talks will get an automatic zero."

"Can't we ask questions?" someone wanted to know. "What if we don't understand something?"

"Then come and ask me. Everybody ready?"

A chorus of murmured noes was the only response.

Mrs. Slater laughed. "Well, good luck then. You've got until break."

Bo skimmed the five pages of word problems. He wondered which question Matthew had written. Probably the one about hockey. It listed a bunch of game scores and asked which team won the championship.

No trick there, Bo thought as he penciled in "Mad City Flyers." *That's Matthew's team, for Pete's sake!*

The other questions were pretty easy, and Bo could almost guess who had written each one. Carrie had probably dreamed up the one about yards of netting needed to sew tutus for a corps de ballet. If it wasn't Carrie, it had to be Jenny. Andrew's was the one about how many soccer cleats are on a playing field. And who else but Rosie, the horse nut, would have even cared about the number of horseshoes worn by a team of Clydesdales? Bo was just double-checking his answers when Matthew tapped his arm with a pencil.

Bo turned his head.

"I know the answer to yours," Matthew whispered.

Bo nodded but said nothing.

"Knowing how you feel about Jim," Matthew continued, "the answer's got to be two."

"Two?" Bo frowned. How could anyone as smart as Matthew come up with two days as an answer?

"As in *too many*," Matthew explained.

"That's a good one." Bo couldn't help grinning.

Mrs. Slater's chair scritched across the floor. She strode swiftly toward them. "All right," she said. "Give me your papers. I can see I'm going to have to separate you boys, aren't I?"

"Mrs. Slater, please! It wasn't Bo's fault. I was just making a joke," Matthew said.

"Talking is talking. And I distinctly heard Bo say *two*."

Bo groaned. How could he be so dumb? His answer came in a name—Jim Harmon. All Matthew did was mention the guy, and Bo's brains flew right out the window.

Mrs. Slater whisked their papers off their desks. She was about to rip them up, but Bo shot out of his seat and stopped her.

"Please," he said, "I know my grade won't count, but I just want to know if I could have made the team."

"What about you?" Mrs. Slater asked Matthew.

He shrugged, refusing to look up. "I still don't think Bo should get a zero," he muttered.

"I'm sorry, boys. But fair is fair." She glanced at Bo's answers and shook her head. "That's too bad. It looks like a perfect paper."

Bo bit his lip and shuffled back to his seat. Several of the kids in the front row offered him smiles of sympathy. "Tough break," one whispered.

Bo nodded glumly. He could have made the math team. Should have, if not for Jim Harmon. Just hearing Matthew say his name had made Bo forget Mrs. Slater's warning. That wasn't *Matt's* fault; it was Jim's, the creep. And now Bo had to explain a big, fat zero to Dad. He could just imagine what Dad would say, too. No more gymnastics!

If only I'd used Eric's name or Jed's in the problem, Bo thought, *nothing would have happened. Why, oh why, did I write about Jim?*

Ironing It Out

BO TRUDGED UPHILL from the bus stop, crunching through dry leaves that blanketed the gutter. He shivered inside his windbreaker and hunched his shoulders against the nippy October wind. What was he going to tell Mom about not making the math team and getting a zero for a grade? That it was all Jim Harmon's fault?

Somehow he doubted that she'd believe him.

And somehow he doubted that she'd keep the bad news to herself.

As he opened the back door, he could hear the "Guiding Light" theme song, blaring from the TV. It stopped abruptly. Mom called out a greeting from the den.

Bo was surprised to see her ironing, something almost as rare as sticking to her diet. The scent of spray starch hung in the air and made him cough.

"Poor Philip," Mom said with a sniff. "He's always got such problems." Philip, Bo knew, was a character on her soap.

"Poor *me*," he mumbled.

"What was that?"

"Nothing," Bo said. "Chris'per's gone?"

"How'd you guess?"

Bo pointed to the iron. He'd heard Mom use his brother as a reason for not doing a lot of things. Cleaning house was one of them. Ironing was another. Dad always said that was some excuse. But Bo knew it wasn't; it was the honest-to-goodness truth! There was no way anyone could work with Christopher around.

"So where is he, anyway?"

"He made a new little friend down the street," Mom said. "They'll walk him home around supper time."

"You didn't forget I have practice, did you?"

"Today's only Wednesday."

Bo sighed. "Don't you remember? The girls' team needs the gym for a meet tomorrow. Anyway, you've got that parents' meeting."

"That's tonight? You're kidding!" She shook her head and set the iron on its heel. "Well, I guess I'll have to bring Christopher. Dad's working late."

"He's always working late."

"It's not easy for him, joining a new law firm," Mom said. "There's a lot of pressure."

"That's *his* fault," Bo muttered. "I still don't see why he had to leave the old one."

Mom sighed. "We've tried to explain it, dear. Don't you remember that little talk we had about quality of life?"

Bo nodded glumly. He remembered just fine. That's all Dad had talked about for months—the clean Wisconsin air, safe neighborhoods, good old American values. Bo guessed that stuff was important to Mom and Dad. But what about the quality of *his* life? Didn't that count for anything?

Back in California, everything felt easy, natural. He didn't have to try so hard. And even if there *was* Mickey Schrader, at least *he* didn't make things like the math-team qualifier backfire in Bo's face. Here, it seemed the harder he tried, the more he messed up. It wasn't fair. Bo sighed and headed for the kitchen in search of a snack.

Mom called after him, but he did not reply. *Let her worry about Philip,* he thought. *She doesn't care how I feel.*

Bo ransacked the refrigerator, but there was nothing good. It figured. Today was going from bad to worse. He should have expected it. He searched the cabinets in vain, slamming doors in exasperation.

As if Jim Harmon wasn't bad enough, now he had

to worry about Christopher being in the gym, too. He doubted that his brother would sit still in the parents' meeting. More than likely, he'd be tearing all over the place. Bo would never hear the end of it. Especially from Jim Harmon. Having a jerky brother was just the kind of thing Jim would make a big deal of. . . .

"Am I supposed to starve to death or what?" he yelled, and jumped when Mom answered from right behind him, "Take an apple."

"Mo-om!"

"What's wrong with an apple?"

"You gave me one for lunch, that's what!" Bo said. "You *always* give me one for lunch, and I'm sick of apples."

Mom laid her hand on his shoulder. He pulled away. "Sounds to me like something else is on your mind," she said.

Bo scowled. "Maybe there is and maybe there isn't. Why should I tell you?"

Mom sighed and rubbed her forehead. "Because I'm on your side, remember?" she said at last. "So, out with it. What happened at school?"

Bo shoved his hands into his pockets and eyed the floor. One of Christopher's round Tinkertoys lay nearby. With the side of his foot, Bo shot it like a hockey puck across the shiny vinyl. Matthew would have loved it.

"Bo! Tell me!" Mom demanded.

"Nothing happened. Nothing! *Zero,* okay?" There. He'd said it. Kind of.

"Well, fine. Suit yourself. I'll be in the den." She padded off in her stocking feet without stopping to pick up the Tinkertoy.

Bo stood alone in the kitchen, listening to the *clunkety-clunk* of the icemaker. At last he tagged after her. "Okay, you want to know?" he said. "I'll tell you."

Mom looked up from her ironing. She did not seem surprised.

"I didn't make the math team, that's what."

"Well," Mom said, "I'm sure you did your best. That's what counts."

"I did do my best, only it *doesn't* count. That's the problem."

Mom shook her head. "You lost me, Bo."

"It's like this," he began, and explained the whole, rotten deal, from beginning to end. "I had a hundred percent. I could have made it, don't you see? Except for dumb old Jim."

"I should think you'd be mad at Matthew," Mom said.

"He's my friend, for Pete's sakes! Why should I be mad at him?"

Mom's blond eyebrows met in the middle, but she said nothing. She just stared at him as if he were speaking Martian. At last she asked, "Well, what are you going to do about the zero?"

"Do? I don't know. What *can* I do?" He handed Mom a hanger and considered his options. It had never occurred to him that there were any. But now . . . "Maybe I'll ask Mrs. Slater if I can do something for extra credit," he suggested. "Do you think that would work?"

"It's sure worth a try."

Bo sucked in a deep breath and let it slowly slip away. "Thanks, Mom. I-I'm sorry about before."

She waved his apology away and turned the iron off. Bo helped her carry Dad's shirts upstairs. The smell of his lime aftershave lingered in their room. *Even when he's gone,* Bo thought, *it feels like Dad is here.*

Mom had disappeared into the walk-in closet. Bo hurried after her and tugged on her sleeve. "One more thing," he said. "Do you have to tell Dad about this?"

Mom ruffled his hair and looked thoughtful. Little shivers shot down his spine. "Well, not tonight," she said at last. "And not *ever* if Mrs. Slater lets you do extra credit."

Bo threw his arms around her. He felt the soft crush of velour against his cheek. "Thanks, Mom," he said. "Really."

Later, after Christopher had come home and they

were on the way to Capital, Bo tried to hold on to his gratitude. His brother, however, was making it hard. He was squirting Bo from behind with the mist bottle that Mom kept in the car for cleaning sticky hands.

"Cut it out!" Bo yelled, turning around to grab it.

Christopher ducked and shot back—*ziff! ziff!*—blasting Bo right in the ear.

Bo unfastened his seat belt and lunged over the seat, landing on top of his brother. He jerked the bottle away and flung it into the back of the station wagon.

Mom turned around, spanking the air in vain. The car swerved. Bo bumped his crazy bone against the door handle. He sat up with a howl.

"You two cut it out!" Mom screamed. "You want to get in a crash? You want us all to be killed?"

"He started it," Bo shot back. "What did I do?"

"Get up here," Mom said. Her voice was trembling with rage. Or maybe fear. Bo couldn't tell.

He crawled over into the front seat and refastened his buckle, glaring at Mom. She always took Christopher's side. Always! It wasn't fair. Mom cranked the radio up and they rode the rest of the way to Capital without talking.

As soon at the front wheels hit the curb, Bo hopped out. "The meeting's upstairs," he said. "In the observation place."

"Okay," Mom sighed. She sounded tired. "Maybe Christopher will play with some of those old toys. But, well, you know him."

Bo slammed the door and muttered, "Yeah, and I wish I didn't!"

As he raced along the sidewalk to the gym, he caught a whiff of hickory smoke from some neighbor's chimney. *Fall in Wisconsin,* he thought, *feels more like winter back home in California.* Back home—there it was again. He wondered whether he'd ever think of Madison as home.

With a sigh, he yanked the door open. Tonight the changing room was packed. Jim Harmon was nowhere around. Bo hung his bag up and headed into the gym.

With any luck, Jim wouldn't show his face, Bo thought. With any more luck, neither would Christopher.

10

Taysa

"HEY, GUYS!" Bo said, and sat down to stretch out. He could feel his straddle getting wider week by week. Now his chest was almost on the floor.

"Your pancake's looking good, Ragatz," Phil Bender said. "Think we'll be on the same team for the intersquad meet next week?"

"I hope so." Phil was better than any thirteen-to-fifteen Bo had ever seen. The two of them on the same squad would be hard to beat.

"You seen who Harmon's with?" Phil whistled. "Oh, yeah, I forgot. You're too young to check out foxes."

"Think so? Try me." Bo lay flat on his back and tried to pull his foot to his head. "Anyway, I don't know what you're talking about. Jim's not even here."

"That's what you think. Look over there."

Bo craned his neck to see where Phil was pointing. Standing by the team bulletin board at the other entrance to the gym were Jim and a tall, thin blonde. Her short sweatshirt dress was the color of robins' eggs.

Bo crawled over to Phil.

The older boy jabbed him in the ribs and teased, "What are *you* looking at?"

"Nothing!" She had to be Jim's sister. His big sister. Probably home from college.

"Yeah, I'll bet," Phil said. "Come on. We've got laps to do."

Bo nodded and scrambled to his feet. He jogged halfheartedly around the huge floor-exercise mat, unable to keep pace with Phil's long strides. He slowed even more as he neared Jim.

"Better get going, Jamey," the young woman said to Jim. "I'll be upstairs, at least for a while."

"You're staying? Oh, great!" A smile softened the hard set of Jim's jaw. "I was sure you had to go to the airport." He backed away from her. Then, without looking, he took off at a trot.

Bo saw him coming and weaved, but it was too late. Jim smacked right into him.

Bo went sprawling. His chin scraped against the rough carpet. He grimaced but would not cry out.

I shouldn't have been listening, he thought. *Should have just steered clear. . . . The last thing I*

need is trouble with Jim. He lay face down, waiting
for Jim to move away. But the guy would not budge.

"Hey, Bo, what's with you? You okay?"

Bo rolled over and stared up at Jim in surprise.

"Should I get Jack?"

"No, I'm okay," Bo said. "It's just a carpet burn."
Hesitantly, he accepted Jim's outstretched hand,
half-expecting him to let go. Instead, Jim pulled him
off the mat, saying he was sorry, that he wasn't looking where he was going.

"I wasn't, either," Bo said, rubbing his hands on
his T-shirt. As he headed off to finish his laps, his
stomach was doing flip-flops. Jim was being too nice.
What in the world was he up to? Bo's pulse quickened as Jim sped up and jogged alongside.

As they passed underneath the observation gallery, Bo looked up and waved to Mom and Christopher. Jim's sister was up there, too. She was at
least a head taller than Mom. And a lot thinner.

Bo tried to pull ahead, but Jim was sticking to him
like Super Glue. What was with him, anyway? Was
this all for his sister's benefit? If so, Bo wished she'd
visit more often. "I guess she doesn't come home
much, huh?"

"Who?"

"Your sister," Bo said. "Who else?"

"My sister?"

"Yeah, you know." Bo pointed up toward the
gallery. "She's in college, right?"

"No way." Jim laughed. "Are you kidding? That's my mom."

"Your mom?" Bo tried to make sense of it. "But she's too young . . . too pretty . . . to be somebody's mom," he blurted. He stopped running, but kept walking in circles to cool down.

"Well, I'm not lying," Jim said. "It's 'cause she's a big-deal model."

Bo's eyes widened. "You mean like on magazine covers?"

"Uh-huh."

Bo gazed up at the place where Jim's mom had been framed. Now she was gone. But he could still picture her flowing, golden hair. It reminded him of the soft stuff they put on angels at Christmastime. "Is she on TV, too?" he asked.

"Yeah, sometimes. For junk like shampoo." Jim cocked his head. "Haven't you ever heard of Taysa before?"

Bo shook his head. What would he know about models? "She sure has a neat name!" He repeated it softly to himself. It was nothing like Nancy.

"I suppose now you want to copycatter moms, too," Jim said.

"No, I don't. It's just that your mom's, well, different from mine."

"Different's not better," Jim said quietly, his eyes avoiding Bo's.

Bo blinked in amazement. Did Jim really think

Mom was better than Taysa? Why would he say such a thing? Bo bit his lip, wanting to ask, but Jack was calling them over to the pommel horse.

Just the sight of it made Bo groan. Everyone said the side horse was the monster of the gym. But that was being kind, Bo thought. He was lucky to get his legs around the dumb thing, let alone to keep them straight.

He dawdled until the rest of his squad had lined up, then stood at the end, near the folded-up bleachers.

"Hey," Bender said, "what's with you and Jim Bags? Doing laps together, I see?"

Bo hissed at Phil, "Shhhh! You want him to hear you?"

"What do I care? It's a great name. All the guys think so."

Bo's cheeks flushed. "You guys heard?"

"Couldn't help it," Phil said.

"Do me a favor," Bo said. "Just forget it, okay? He'll kill me if you guys start calling him that! And he's actually being nice for a change."

Tony nudged between Phil and Bo. His huge grin revealed a new mouthful of plastic and metal—and the fact that he'd been listening. "Don't take it personally," he said. "The guy's just happy his mom's around, okay?"

"Too bad she's not here more often, huh?" Phil winked at Bo.

The gym had grown embarrassingly quiet. Jack and the other guys were staring at him and Phil. Bo bit his lip, eyed the mat.

"Okay now," the coach said. "Let's get to work."

"Can't see me!" A familiar voice came from behind the metal stands. Christopher!

Bo cringed. He could see the little blue sneakers climbing higher.

"I see you, Bo. I see you."

Now everyone was staring at him again. Why did Christopher have to open his big mouth and call Bo's name? Now everyone *knew*!

"Christopher, get down from there." Bo's cheeks burned. He wished he were invisible. Maybe if he ignored his brother, Christopher would go away. Maybe Mom would come after him. . . .

"Hey, Ragatz," Jack called. "You'd better get him down before he falls."

Bo sighed. He glared up at the window where Mom had been, but like Taysa, she, too, had disappeared.

"I'll do it," Jim offered.

"You?"

"Sure. Why not?"

"Go ahead," Bo said. "You can have him."

Jim stepped out of line and disappeared behind the bleachers. He came out carrying Christopher piggyback and slid him off gently in the doorway.

"I can do a front roll," Christopher said.

"Chris'per, get out of here! Go find Mom!"

Christopher crouched down, pressed his head to the floor, and flopped to one side.

"Here," Jim said, "let me show you." He demonstrated a perfect forward roll right there in the hallway.

"Can you believe it?" Phil whispered.

"No way," Bo said. He was sure Jim was trying to show him up in front of the guys. Which wasn't hard, because Bo knew that he hadn't exactly been Mr. Nice to Christopher.

Jim's plan was working, too. Except for Eric up on the pommel horse, everyone else was looking at Jim like he was Saint James. At last Jack said, "Okay, Harmon, toddler time is over. Let's see your leg cuts."

Jim patted Christopher on the head. Christopher reached up to give him a hug. And Jim hugged him back!

Bo knew that everyone was laughing at him. Maybe not out loud. But he could see it in their eyes. Jim and Christopher had made him look like a fool, and it was all Mom's fault. Why couldn't she watch him? Where was she, anyway?

Jim jumped up from the mat to a support on the pommels. He swung one leg up and over the horse, then swung the other. He fell into a rhythm—up and over, up and back—with his hands regrasping each time his legs swung past.

"Okay, that's good," Jack said.

Jim nudged back into line beside Bo. "Your brother's kind of cute," he whispered. "What is he? Four?"

Bo nodded and pressed his lips together, holding in the anger that bubbled up without warning. "You want him? You can have him!" he blurted. "I'll even throw in Mom, too. Just give me yours." Ignoring everyone's stares, he stormed off to the changing room.

"It's a deal," Jim called after him.

Yanking his jacket off the hook, Bo flung it over his shoulders and straight-armed the front door. The crisp night air slapped at his face. His eyes burned with tears.

"Hey!" Stu shouted. "Are you all right?"

Bo nodded without turning.

"You coming back?"

Bo wanted to say no. How could he go back in there and face everyone? But when he thought about it, he had no choice. There was nowhere else he wanted to be.

11

Starting Over

THE NEXT DAY Bo walked to Matthew's house after school. The Weilers lived just a block from Orchard Ridge Elementary—two from the adjacent middle school—in a big, old, white house with tall columns in the front. Though Halloween was two weeks away, their porch was already lined with carved pumpkins.

Matthew slammed the door behind them and dropped his backpack in the entry hall. Bo wriggled out of his but held it in his arms.

"Oh, it's okay," Matthew said. "Just throw it anywhere."

Bo set his backpack beside Matthew's and followed him into the kitchen. Mrs. Weiler was flipping some chocolate-chip cookies onto a wire rack.

"Hi, boys," she said. "Help yourselves."

Matthew grabbed a handful. Bo took only two, but wished he'd taken more.

"See wha' I tol' you?" Matthew said, his mouth full. He swallowed hard. "It's like this every day. I swear."

Matthew flopped into a huge beanbag chair in the family room and scooched over to make room for Bo.

"Beats apples," Bo said. "Thanks for inviting me."

"Yeah, like I never did before?" Matthew jabbed Bo's arm playfully.

"I know. I know. I just get so worried about not getting my homework done. And then there's gym practice."

"So?" Matthew said. "A kid's got to have *some* fun, right?" He turned his palm up.

"Right!" Bo said, slapping it.

Matthew chomped down another cookie. "So what did you have to talk to Mrs. Slater about?" he asked.

"Extra credit," Bo said. "To make up for that zero in math."

Matthew screwed his face up and scrunched deeper into the beanbag chair.

"Hey, I'm not blaming you," Bo said.

"I know. You're too nice." Matthew munched thoughtfully on his third cookie. "I guess your dad was pretty mad, huh? Is he going to make you quit the team?"

"He doesn't even know about it. Mom's not going to tell, either, if I can do something to pull up my grade."

"What did Mrs. Slater say?"

"She said I could write twenty-five story problems by next Friday. You can do it, too," Bo said, "if you want to."

"I don't know." Matthew shook his head. "It seems like a lot of work. Especially with 'Pioneers' due next Friday, too."

"Pioneers!" Bo had almost forgotten about their creative problem-solving assignment on the Old West. He had kept up with the diary entries and trail decisions. No problem. But it was the research paper on the pony express that troubled him now.

"Well," he said, "I really don't have a choice. I'll just find a way to get everything done, that's all."

"Good luck. I think I'll take my zero."

"Not me," Bo said. "No way."

Bo eyed Matthew's last cookie longingly. Had there ever been a time when Mom had baked chocolate chips—or anything else, for that matter?

Matthew grinned. "Here," he said, giving Bo the whole thing. "You're gonna need all the energy you can get."

"Gee, thanks!" Bo nibbled around the edge, savoring each bite. "Did Eric tell you what Jim did last night?" he asked at last.

"Yeah. I don't believe it. And he said you ran out in the middle of practice, too."

Bo nodded glumly. "Pretty dumb, huh? I don't know. It just got to me, him playing kissy-face with Christopher. Everybody must have thought I was a real jerk."

"I doubt it. Jim's the jerk. He was probably just trying to get to you."

"I thought so, too," Bo said, "but you know, it seemed like he kind of got off on playing big brother."

Eric breezed in and flipped the TV on. "You two talking about Jim?" he asked.

"Yeah, who else?" Bo said.

"Aw, give him a break." Eric thumbed absently through the *TV Guide.* "The guy's just lonely."

"Well, it's his own fault," Matthew said. "Bo never tried to be his enemy, you know."

Eric turned the set off. "Maybe not. But you sure do get him going. And that name you made up—Jim Bags!" Eric laughed. "Great way to make friends, right?"

Bo scowled. "Yeah, well. It just slipped out. I didn't know you guys were going to keep saying it."

"Maybe we will," Eric said, "and maybe we won't."

Matthew crawled to the sofa, grabbed a pillow,

and blasted Eric in the face with it. "Just get out of here if you're not on Bo's side," he said. "Traitor!"

Bo's side. Was that how the guys on the team saw it, that they had to choose between him and Jim? Or was it just Matthew? Too bad Ruiz wasn't there to give one of his pep talks. That would bring the team together.

"Bye, girls!" Bo looked up to see Eric paste on a sticky-sweet smile, wave, and disappear down the hall.

"Good riddance. Now"—Matthew sat cross-legged at Bo's feet—"where were we, anyway? Oh, yeah. You were saying how creepy-nice Jim was being."

"Yeah," Bo said. "Even before the thing with Christopher he was just being unreal. *Too* nice, if you know what I mean."

"Like he wanted something?"

Bo considered the possibility, then shook his head. "No. It was more like . . . oh, I don't know. He was just, well, happy. Tony says it's because his mom was there." He remembered the way Jim had smiled at Taysa, and chuckled softly. "No wonder! She's really something!"

"Yeah? What's so special about her?" Matthew asked. "Eric never said a thing."

Bo told him.

"Big wow." Matthew rolled onto his side and braced his head with his hand. "Anyway, who'd want a famous mom like that? She's probably never around. And then when she is, dumb girls are probably bugging her for her autograph.''

"But my mom—"

"Yeah, I know. You told me a zillion times," Matthew said. "So what if she doesn't bake cookies and junk? So what if she's kinda fat? At least she's there!"

Bo said nothing. He hadn't thought of that. Maybe Matthew had a point. It would sure explain Jim's good mood. It might even explain what Jim meant about "different's not better." He wondered. . . .

"Bo?" Matthew snapped his fingers in front of Bo's face. "You still there?"

"What? Oh, yeah." Bo refocused, shaking off his daze. "I was just thinking. Maybe I should kind of start over with Jim. You know, be nicer. What do you think?"

Matthew shrugged. "Can't hurt, I guess."

"It can't, can it?" He promised himself he'd start right away, at the intersquad meet Tuesday night.

Jack had said the meet was no big deal, that it was just another kind of practice. But he was wrong. It was a big deal to Bo. And to Jim. And to the rest of the guys, too.

Bo could tell because when Tuesday night finally came, parents filled the gallery window and spilled downstairs onto the mats. Jack and Stu had to unfold the bleachers and herd the parents all into one place.

It was the only way to make room for the team to tumble.

Bo went to change while Mom, Dad, and Christopher found seats. The dressing room looked like a hurricane had just blown through. Tennies and tube socks, jackets and gym bags—all were strewed crazily about. It was as if no one knew what hooks were for.

Bo shook his head and resisted the urge to pair up the shoes. Let everyone else worry about it later. His would be zipped safely inside his new red-and-blue gym bag, hanging on the wall.

Bo nestled his shoes in the bag, sole side out, taking care not to crinkle his extra-credit problems and pony express report. They were both almost done. He had been carrying them everywhere, writing a problem here, a paragraph there. No way would he leave everything until Thursday night.

"You ready to get beat?"

Bo whirled about to see Jim standing in the doorway, swinging his old gym bag back and forth. Jim let go, and it flew across the room, hit the wall, and flopped onto the bench beside Bo.

He picked up the bag and hung it beside his.

"What did you do that for?" Jim said.

Bo shrugged apologetically. "Sorry. Guess it's just a habit." Then, "Hey, look at that! Our gym bags are twins!"

"Yeah, I thought you'd like that. Anyway, I squished a jelly doughnut on my new one."

"You did?" Bo started to laugh until he saw how sad Jim looked. "Gee, that's too bad."

"Like you really mean it," Jim said. "Well, who cares? I still have my lucky grips. That's what counts."

Lucky grips! The whole idea was ridiculous. Bo remembered his promise to be nice to Jim, but he couldn't help asking, "You don't really believe those things make a difference, do you? I mean, what if you lost them or something?"

Jim glared at Bo. "Wouldn't *you* like to find out," he said, dangling the grips before Bo's eyes. "Me lose these babies? Dream on, Shrimpboat. Dream on." He backed toward the gym, smirking.

Bo sighed. Why couldn't he even ask a simple question without Jim getting mad?

Switcheroo

PHIL BENDER POKED his head in and told Bo to hurry up. "We've got a squad to beat!" he said.

As Bo entered the gym, he scanned the crowd. Mom and Dad were sitting next to the Weilers. Matthew was stuck beside Christopher. There were other people he'd never seen before, but no sign of Taysa. Not yet, anyway.

Bo joined the other guys for group warm-ups. They really looked like a team tonight, he thought. Everyone had on gold step-ins—not wimpy, light blue ones like his California team had worn—and long, white stretch pants. Everyone except Denny. He was wearing baggy, gray sweatpants because his mom hadn't had time to shorten his whites. At least Mom had managed to hem Bo's. But it was humiliating, being eleven and too short for the smallest size.

Jack told the parents that he would be judging, while Stu flashed the scores. "I tried to tell the boys that this meet was just a practice," he said, "but I can see from the turnout how important it is to them. And to you. I'm glad they're taking competition so seriously. However—"

The coach paused and seemed to be scanning the crowd for someone. He scratched his head, sighed, and pressed on. "Well, anyway, I hope you parents will encourage the boys to compete against themselves, to set goals and try to meet them. That's what winning's all about, really. And if they get ribbons and medals in the process, well, that's gravy."

Up in the stands Mom was nodding emphatically. Bo rolled his eyes. It sure sounded as if she'd talked to Jack—and after she'd promised not to!

Bo finished warming up, and as Jack announced the squads, a zillion moths started flapping about in his stomach. Squad A included Phil, Bo, Jed, Eric, and Denny. Pete Carboni, Dave Payton, Tony, Jim, and Andy Thayer, a new nine-year-old from Milwaukee, were on Squad B.

This is it, Bo told himself. His pulse quickened.

The first event was floor exercise.

Jim was the last guy up on his squad. He stood in the far corner of the spring floor and signaled the coach by raising his hand. Jack nodded. Jim licked his lips, lifted his arms, and began his first tumbling pass.

His front handspring progressed smoothly into a forward roll, and he remembered to face outward on his cartwheels (unlike Denny, who lost five-tenths of a point on that alone). But his back extension roll didn't quite go through to a handstand. His scale—a balancing position with one leg extended backward—looked almost wobbly!

The final pass included a powerful round off–back handspring and a high straight jump. Jim thrust out his chest, played to the judge.

Bo gulped as Stu flashed an 8.9, the highest score on Jim's squad.

Now it was Bo's turn. So far Phil was high man on their squad with an 8.7.

Bo decided to start from the near corner so Jack couldn't compare his routine's tracings with Jim's. Ruiz had told him that was the smart bet, and Bo figured he ought to know.

He flagged the judge, awaited the nod. His heart was pounding in his ears as he began his first pass. He hit the front handspring squarely, stood it up, and moved smoothly into the handstand and forward roll. Momentum and habit swept him along from trick to trick. He hardly had to think at all!

In the last corner, he moved into his pancake, touching his chest to the mat. *Finally! I can go all the way down!* His scale was solid, his round off—

back handspring without breaks. Bo grinned as he thrust his arms upward, triumphant.

When Stu flashed a 9.0, Bo punched the air with his fist, smiling broadly. He sneaked a look at Jim.

Jim's arms were folded across his chest, his eyes intent upon the crowd in the bleachers. He seemed more interested in finding someone than in Bo's score. If he was looking for Taysa, she still wasn't there.

Next came pommel horse, Bo's nightmare apparatus. Jim's long legs showed off well as he swung through the routine, traveling from one end of the horse to the other. Jack rewarded him with a 9.1.

During his set, Bo could feel his thighs graze the horse on each leg cut. He tried to fake it by bending them slightly, but he was sure Jack would notice. His long white pants already bagged in the knees; they wouldn't hide much.

Sure enough. Bo dropped behind with an 8.6.

Phil slapped him on the back. "Don't worry. That was your worst, right? We'll get it back."

Still rings was third. Jim made a big show of strapping his lucky grips on and clapping the excess chalk off. Bo held his breath, wondering whether Jim could repeat that flawless routine he'd thrown the first night of practice.

It looked close, except for two hops on the landing. Jack called it an 8.9.

Bo sucked in a steadying breath. Stu's hands

gripped his waist for the lift. "Go for it, man!" he whispered.

Bo did, but somehow his timing felt off from the very start. He wished he could begin again, but knew he couldn't. He tried to shrug off the 8.4 Jack gave him, but quick math showed Jim almost a full point ahead. Darn! The guy was incredible. Either that or incredibly lucky.

Jim smirked at Bo, waving his grips as if to prove his case.

Goose bumps crept down Bo's arms. He tried to ignore Jim by pacing back and forth, awaiting his turn to vault. The two squads were well matched, Bo thought. Not nearly the runaway Phil had predicted.

The new kid, Andy Thayer, and Denny were neck and neck. And the two freshmen, Phil and Pete, were turning in scores just under Bo's and Jim's. Tony was making up for Dave's slack on Squad B, while Jed and Eric's scores fell consistently between Tony and Dave's. *If I don't make up the difference,* Bo thought, *who will?*

Vault, he knew, wasn't an event to pin his hopes on. It was always over too fast; there was no time to make up for mistakes. But if he hit the board just right . . . well, anything was possible.

Jim tore down the runway, smacked the springboard, and flew over the horse. He had good extension and an even better postflight. Bo was sure that he'd landed at least his own height from the horse. The vault was good for a 9.0.

Bo flagged the judge. His feet pounded toward the mat. If only his legs were longer! If only he could *move!*

The board loomed. He hit it dead center, reached for the horse. His heels were up, his legs extended. *Squat through! Fly!*

Bo dropped over the horse like a stone. *Darn!* No distance. If only he were taller . . .

Stu flashed an 8.5.

"What am I down?" Bo asked Phil. "I've just got to beat that guy!"

Phil closed one eye, ticking his head from side to side as he added the scores. "One-point-four," he said. "But don't sweat it. I've seen you on bars, man. You can do it!"

"You think so?"

"Absolutely!" Phil slapped Bo five and waved him off to the parallel bars.

The other guys' routines were a blur. Bo practiced his moves in his head. He tried to blot out everything else.

Jim threw an 8.0. He'd bobbled his dismount, rolled too early out of his shoulder stand. This was Bo's chance!

He asked Stu to help him lower the bars and adjust them inward. That's just what he *didn't* need—to fall through on his shoulder stand. Then he blew out a deep breath and charged the springboard.

Determination steeled his L-support. He knew he could win an extra tenth of virtuosity by pressing to a handstand, then lowering to his shoulders, and still another tenth by swinging to another handstand on the dismount. Both were worth a try; he had nothing to lose. Not anymore.

The chalkboard read 9.1.

Bo heard Matthew's whoop above the polite applause and blushed. He'd narrowed his difference with Jim to three-tenths. Only high bar remained.

Fortunately, that was his best event.

Unfortunately, it was Jim's as well.

Bo's team was up first. Phil turned in a 9.0. "That ought to help," he whispered as he passed Bo at the chalk box.

Bo signaled Jack, got the nod, and stood beneath the high bar. He looked up, licking his lips, and felt Stu's hands around his waist.

Here goes, he thought as he reached for the bar.

Two big pumps and Bo knew the routine would click. He'd never gotten such height before, had never kept his legs so straight on the single-leg shoot. Bo felt as if some great Olympian—Peter Vidmar, maybe, or Mitch Gaylord—had seized control of his body, as if he, Bo Ragatz, were merely along for the ride.

He sailed under the bar, then up, out, and away. The arch and landing were perfect; he could feel it! His arms split the air in triumph.

Jack raised his eyebrows and nodded once, then he mouthed a score to Stu.

Bo's heart pounded in his ears. He heard the crowd gasp and applaud even louder. Then he saw why.

"Nine-point-six?" Bo turned to Phil, afraid his eyes were playing tricks. That score was considered perfect in his class of competition. Only virtuosity points could inch it toward the ultimate—10.

"You got it!" Phil came forward, followed by Jed, Eric, and Denny, clapping him on the back and congratulating him.

"Don't look now," Phil said. "But I think Harmon's losing it."

As Jim took his place under the bar, one of the older guys from the other squad called, "Hey, Jim Bags! Don't get mad, get even!"

Bo bit his knuckle. He was in for it now!

Jim pursed his lips, lowered his brows. His face was chiseled with determination. His eyes were as hard as steel. He clapped his grip-covered hands and waited for the lift. As he grasped the bar, his long legs pumped upward. He had power. Bo couldn't deny it.

His routine was flawless as far as Bo could tell.

There wasn't a break, either in rhythm or form. It was going to be close.

At last came Jim's score—8.9. Bo was as surprised as Jim.

"Eight-point-nine?" Jim said to Jack, his voice rising. "What was wrong with that?"

"You didn't regrip on the back swing," Jack said. He sounded apologetic. "Mandatory seven-tenths deduction."

Jim ripped his grips free. The Velcro made a terrible, tearing sound. "I'll bet!" he said, and bolted across the gym.

He slowed near the bleachers and looked the crowd over one more time. Then he shook his head and disappeared into the changing room.

One part of Bo thought about running after him. He'd tell Jim, "Maybe next time you'll win. You did great. Really." But the rest of him wanted to stay there and soak in the moment.

Let him go, he thought. *He's a bad sport anyway.*

"Hey, Bo! Congratulations! We won—natch!— and you were high scorer," Jed said.

Phil whistled. "Boy, fifty-three-point-two! What do you do for an encore?"

Bo shrugged. "I don't know. Fifty-three-point-three?"

"Okay, A Squad!" Jack said. "Everybody upstairs! The juice boxes are on me." He tousled Bo's hair.

"Nice work, Ragatz. Think you can throw that at the Red Gym meet come Sunday?"

"I sure hope so," Bo said.

"You do and I'll bet you bring home your first medal." Jack glanced at the numbers on his clipboard, shaking his head in disbelief. "Ruiz sure was right about you! Maybe *we* ought to think about having a mandatory practice year, huh?"

Before Bo could reply, he was swept up by the others. He turned to catch a glimpse of Mom and Dad coming down from the stands. Christopher was sitting on Dad's shoulders.

Matthew had pushed ahead of the Weilers and was giving Bo the thumbs-up sign. "Way to go!" he called. "You, too, Eric!"

"I'll be up in a minute," Bo told Phil. "Save me a juice box." He squeezed free of the crush of bodies.

Mom rushed over and kissed him.

"Ah, come on, Mom. Not here, okay?" Bo said.

Dad unwrapped Christopher's arms from around his head and set him on the floor. "You did great, Bozer! But you know, you've gotta work on that pommel horse. That thing's a real bear!"

Bo nodded glumly.

"So where's this Taysa person, this model you were telling me about?" Mom asked. "I know you said she was at that parents' meeting, but I just can't place her."

"Yeah," Matthew chimed in. "I thought you said she'd be here."

"Well, she's not," Bo said. "I just figured . . ." His voice trailed off. Had Jim figured the same thing? Maybe *that's* why he was so mad. Maybe it wasn't about his score at all.

"I'll be right back," he said.

Matthew called after him as he dashed toward the changing room. But Bo didn't stop. Couldn't. He'd have to explain later.

Jim wasn't there—and his gym bag was gone, too.

Bo sighed, grabbing his own bag. It sure felt light. He frowned, then zipped it open. Inside was a strange, red-striped T-shirt with a blue alligator on the breast pocket.

"Oh, no! Jim's got *my* bag!"

Then another thought struck him. Inside the bag were his shoes . . . and his homework!

13

Waiting Game

"I'M SURE IT WAS just an accident," Mom said in the car on the way home. "Just call him. You'll see."

"Oh, don't worry," Bo said. "I'm gonna call him all right."

"Now, Bo," Mom said, "it's not like he took your only pair of shoes. I don't know why you're taking this so hard. Mix-ups happen."

Bo eyed Jim's look-alike gym bag. It lay on the floor, deflated. He wondered whether he should tell her about the homework. All he needed right now was the Responsibility Lecture.

"Yeah," Bo said. "I guess these things happen."

Silence stretched between them. Bo flipped the radio on, tuned in a hard-rock station.

Mom turned it to soft rock, then abruptly clicked

it off. "It was nice of your dad to make it, don't you think?"

"Uh-huh," Bo said.

"I don't think he's ever really seen how good you are."

"Mmmm-hmmm." He had to get those extra-credit problems and his report back before Friday. But how? If he didn't, Dad would never let him compete in the Red Gym meet. He was sure of that.

Mom was nudging his shoulder. "What?" he said. "Oh, sorry. I didn't hear you."

"Obviously. I said I bet you appreciated Dad taking Christopher home right after the meet."

"Yeah. I did."

"Well," Mom said, "it would be nice if you mentioned it when we get home."

Bo nodded. But somehow it was hard to think about even facing Dad, now that his homework was missing.

By the time Bo had a chance to phone Jim, it was after nine-thirty. Dad was finally holed up in the den with the contents of his briefcase. And Mom, he thought, was upstairs, tucking Christopher in for the eighty-eleventh time.

Now was his chance.

He had dialed only half of the numbers when Mom sneaked up from behind. She demanded to know why he was bothering someone at this "ungodly hour."

Bo hung up the phone. "Please, Mom, I've just gotta call Jim!"

"It can wait until tomorrow." She stood there with her hands on her hips, as unmovable as the Great Wall of China.

The Great Wall of China? Hadn't he seen David Copperfield, the magician, pass right through the wall on TV? Bo smiled. Maybe there *was* a way around Mom after all.

"No, it can't wait," he said. "Not really. See, my homework was in my gym bag. You know, my report for 'Pioneers' and the extra-credit stuff for the math. I've got to get it back, otherwise . . ."

"I'm beginning to get the picture. All right. Make the call. But be sure to apologize."

Bo grinned and redialed the number. "Don't worry, Mom. I was going to anyway."

Someone answered on the third ring. "Harmon residence." The woman sounded a lot older than Taysa.

"I'm sorry to call so late, but is Jim there? I really need to talk to him."

"Little Jim?" the woman asked.

"Uh, yes, I guess so. The one who does gymnastics." Somehow Bo had never thought of Jim as little.

"Just one moment, please. I'll see if the car's home yet."

The car? Bo thought. Wasn't it easier just to look for Jim?

The phone fell silent for several minutes. Bo watched Mom puttering around the kitchen, wiping off countertops, scouring the sink. He could smell the Comet all the way across the room. Mom's reasons for being there were quickly running out. Bo wished she'd stop pretending to be busy. He was sure she only wanted to listen in.

"I'm sorry to keep you waiting," came the woman's voice. "Jim will be right with you."

"Jim? Hey, it's me, Bo."

"Oh, hi."

"Sorry your mom didn't make the meet. Guess she had to work, huh?" Bo wished he could take back the words the instant they'd left his lips.

Jim sighed. "You called to tell me that?"

"Uh, no, n-not exactly," Bo stammered.

"You think you're better than me, just because your whole family came?"

"No, I don't. I just felt bad—"

"Oh, save it," Jim said. "I know what you guys think of me. What do I care? I don't need you and I don't need them. I don't need anybody. All I need to do is win."

Bo couldn't believe that he actually felt sorry for the guy. "You'll win," he said. "You would have. Really. It was just a dumb thing, that regrip deduction."

"That's easy for you to say. It worked out great for you, didn't it?"

Bo gulped. "Look, that's not why I called. See, I think you've got my gym bag." What was he saying? He *knew* Jim had it. "And, well, the problem is, my shoes are in there and—"

"I'll bring them to practice on Thursday, okay?"

"Well, see, it's more than my shoes," Bo said. "There's some homework and it's due—"

"No problem," Jim cut in. "I'll tell our house-keeper to mail it to you."

"Do you think it'd get here in time? By Friday?" Bo was afraid he'd say too much.

"How should *I* know? Want me to bring it Thursday night? That's before Friday, right?"

"Yes, but . . . Look, it's really important you don't forget it, okay?"

"Why would I forget it?" Jim sounded annoyed.

Bo shrugged and said nothing.

"I mean if you don't trust me to—"

"I trust you, okay? It's just that if you forget it, I can't be in the Red Gym meet," Bo blurted.

"What?"

Bo wished he could stuff his words back down his throat. What was the matter with him tonight, anyway?

"Nothing," he said, and hoped Jim really hadn't heard after all. "Just . . . please . . . remember it on Thursday, okay?"

"Sure, Shrimpboat," Jim said. "I'll remember. I'm re-e-al good at remembering."

"Thanks." Bo tried to ignore the way Jim dragged out the *real.* "I'll see you at practice. Be there early, okay?"

As he hung up the phone, his eyes met Mom's. They mirrored all his worst fears. She didn't need to say a word. Like it or not, Jim had him playing a waiting game until their next practice.

14

Last Chance

BO RACED into the gym Thursday night at ten minutes to six. Jed, Eric, and Tony were already there. They were goofing around with a beanbag. Jack would shout their heads off if he saw them. Bo wondered where he was. But not for long.

"Ragatz!" the coach bellowed. His voice rattled the glass window between the gym and the office. "Get in here and pick up your warm-up shirt!"

"Coming!"

Jack slid the window open and passed Bo his white sweatshirt. It said CAPITAL down the right sleeve and GYMNASTICS down the left. Bo extended the arms and laughed. If a strong wind ever blew through the gym, he was sure to sail away. The sweatshirt was that big.

"Gee, Jack, uh, thanks," he said.

100

"Don't forget it on Sunday."

"Sunday?"

Jack sighed. "The Red Gym meet? Sound familiar?"

"Oh, yeah. Sure." How could he think about Sunday? If Jim didn't show up with his homework, the day might as well not exist.

Bo stuffed the sweatshirt into his gym bag—actually, Jim's old one—and joined the others for warm-ups. Eric scooted toward him. "Matt told me what Harmon did," he said. "You think he's gonna show?"

Bo sat in a straddle and bent to one side, laying his body on his leg. Matthew! That wise guy had been driving Bo crazy, taking bets on whether or not Jim would come through. Bo almost wished he'd never told him what had happened—except that Matthew had promised to treat at Dairy Queen with his winnings.

From Mrs. Slater's class alone Matt had already collected five dollars and sixty cents. For once, she hadn't caught him. That was the good news. The bad news was that when Matthew told everyone about Jim's crummy attitude, most kids sympathized with Bo, but bet against him anyway.

"He'd better show up," Bo said. "Or else."

"Or else what?"

"Or else I can't go to the meet."

"Oh." Eric sounded like he was expecting a different answer. "You mean you're not going to punch him out?"

"Who, me?" Bo laughed. "I'll be *mad* if he doesn't show up, but not crazy!"

"Yeah. I see your point. Well, good luck. We all hope he brings it."

Bo nodded glumly. He completed his warm-ups, one eye on the clock. What if Jim were sick? It was already quarter after; usually he wasn't this late.

Stu was calling off the guys in each squad. Bo moved numbly toward the pommel horse. He was following Eric.

"Ragatz!" Stu called from the vaulting horse. "Hey! You're with me!"

"I am?" Bo shrugged apologetically and hustled over.

He tried to keep his mind on vaulting, but trying wasn't good enough. Not tonight.

"What was that, Ragatz?" Stu demanded. "You looked like a flying jellyfish!"

All the guys laughed.

Bo's cheeks went hot. "Sorry, Stu. Want me to try it again?"

"Not that! Just give me a plain old layout like you used to."

Bo nodded, but as he turned to go back down the runway, he saw Jim, standing near the changing room. He started to wave him over, but Jack beat him to it.

Bo groaned as Jim headed for the pommels. He went back to try his vault again. Stu was quick to point out that it was no improvement. Bo might as well have stayed home, he said. "Even *you* can't afford to waste a practice right before a meet."

The next two and a half hours seemed more like twelve. But at last Bo bolted for the changing room, right after Jim. He caught Jim's arm; Jim spun about.

"All right," Bo said, "where is it?"

"Where's what?"

"You know what. My homework. My shoes. My gym bag."

Jim slapped his own cheek in mock dismay. "I *knew* I forgot something."

"Come on, Jim." Bo chuckled nervously. "You're kidding me. I mean, you *did* promise to bring my gym bag, remember?"

"Did I?" Jim shrugged. "Well, as you can see, I brought my new one."

Bo eyed the bench where a gold-and-black bag lay. It had a purplish stain on the side pocket.

"I see there really was a jelly doughnut," Bo said.

"I told you there was."

"Yeah, you told me a lot of things." Bo paced back and forth. "Now what am I going to do?"

"Search me," Jim said. "Didn't your homework come in the mail today?"

Bo shook his head.

"Well, you ought to get it tomorrow then."

"Too late," Bo muttered, "and you know it. What about the rest of my stuff? Didn't you bring *anything*?"

"Go ahead and look."

Jack poked his head in the door. "Hey, you two," he said, "I hate to break this up but I need to see Harmon in the office."

"Right now?" Jim asked.

"If you want your sweatshirt before Sunday," Jack replied.

"Okay, I'm coming." Jim turned to Bo. "I'll bring your stuff next week. Cross my heart." He flashed Bo a phony smile and hurried after Jack.

Bo pounded his fist on the bench. Now what was he going to do? He eyed Jim's gold gym bag and wondered whether Jim was just teasing. Hadn't he challenged Bo to look inside? Maybe he *should* . . . just to be sure.

Zipping open the bag, he pawed through the contents. There was nothing there but a Yosemite wallet, a comb, a pair of jeans, and Jim's grips. What had he expected?

Bo started to rezip the bag. One of the Velcro straps was hanging out. *Jim and his stupid lucky grips!* Bo thought. *How would he like it if they'd been in* his *bag and I didn't bring* them *back?*

Bo's hand shook as it reached for the strap. He was going to tuck it inside. That's all he was going to do. But somehow his hand just wouldn't let go.

In an instant, the grips were in another bag: Jim's old red-and-blue one—the one Bo had brought to exchange for his own.

Bo's heartbeat was tripping over itself. He couldn't believe what he had just done. It was like a dream. He could hear some guys laughing in the hall. Maybe Jim was out there, too.

Bo flung the look-alike bag over his shoulder and nudged past them without saying good-bye. Then he hustled out the door and into Mom's waiting car.

Facing the
Horrible Giant

"HI, HONEY. How was practice?" Mom squinted at Bo in the dim parking-lot light. She flipped on the overhead and worried aloud about how pale he looked. "Are you sure you're not coming down with something?"

Bo shook his head, struggling to get words past the knot in his throat. "Must be chalk dust," he said. Pale? That was a laugh. He felt like he was burning up. Why couldn't Mom hurry up and get out of here? Jim might come tearing after him any second.

"Chalk dust, really?" Mom reached out to feel his forehead.

Bo pulled away. "Mo-om! I told you I'm okay. Can't we just go home?"

She shrugged and turned off the light. "If you

say so." They were cruising down McKenna when she finally asked, "Hey! Did Jim bring your things?"

"Nope."

"You're kidding."

Bo shook his head. "I should've known. He probably did it on purpose. Mickey Schrader would've."

Mom sighed. "Well, I suppose there are always going to be Mickey Schraders no matter where you live. The point is, what are *you* going to do?"

"Extra credit on the extra credit?" Bo managed a weak smile. "I kind of doubt it."

"Maybe if I write Mrs. Slater a note—"

"But what about Dad?" Bo fought back tears. Dad was harder than the Great Wall of China. Even David Copperfield couldn't get past him.

"Well . . . I really hate to keep things from him." Mom sighed again. "But it's not like you didn't do the work. It'll just be a little late." She patted Bo's leg. "Don't worry. We'll work it out."

Bo blew out a long, slow breath. He felt as if he'd been holding the same one all the way home from Capital.

"Thanks, Mom," he said as they both hung up their jackets. He gave her a quick kiss. "I'm going to bed now."

"Don't I get one?"

Bo whirled about to see Dad filling the mudroom doorway. His eyes fought to avoid his father's. "Oh, sure." Bo delivered the kiss and kept right on going.

"Hey, what's with you?" Dad caught his hand and reeled him back.

"Nothing. I'm just tired."

"No wonder! It's after nine. That's no kind of bed-time on a school night. When I was your age, it was dinner, homework, and to bed by eight."

Bo hung his head. *Grandma made you go to bed at eight o'clock when you were eleven? Right, Dad.* Sometimes he thought his father had forgotten how old Bo was. And where was Mom when he needed her? In the kitchen, making a big racket with dishes and silverware. He could hear the freezer door open—probably for some ice cream—and slap shut again. Bo sighed. Leave it to Mom to eat when the going got tough. . . .

"Say!" Dad continued. "You never showed me that pony express report. How about it? It's due tomorrow, isn't it?"

Bo nodded but could not speak.

"Ted," Mom called from the kitchen, "I made you a sundae. Come on in, before the fudge gets gloppy."

"Did you make me one, too?" Bo asked.

"Just Dad. You go on to bed."

Bo's feet hit the stairs before Dad could stop him. He'd never been so glad not to have a hot-fudge sundae in his life. He was just easing his door open when he heard Dad tell Mom he'd be there in a minute. After he read Bo's report.

Bo nudged aside the trail of Matchbox cars Christopher had left on the floor, kicked off his shoes, and crawled under his covers, still wearing his sweats. It smelled like Christopher had wet his bed again, but Bo wasn't about to awaken him.

Closing his eyes, he rolled toward the wall and pretended to be asleep. He could hear Dad's footfalls crushing the carpet, coming closer and closer.

"I know you're awake," Dad whispered. When he sat on the bed, Bo rolled toward him without trying. "This isn't like you, Bo. I want to know what's going on."

"Nothing's going on. I told you. I'm just tired."

"Baloney. You'd keep doing that gymnastics until midnight if they'd let you. Don't give me you're tired. It doesn't wash. Not with me."

Mom had tried. She really had. Even though she didn't like keeping things from Dad, Bo thought. Good old Mom. He bet the hot-fudge sundae had been her way of keeping Dad away. Now Bo guessed there was nothing else to do but tell the truth. And he did, starting with the Math Mess-Up.

"So you see, it's in the mail. That's what Jim says, anyway. And we can't even drive over and get it," he concluded.

Christopher's Mickey Mouse night-light threw Dad's shadow against the wall. He looked like a horrible giant. Bo could see him working his jaw in silence and wished he'd say something—anything! This not knowing was tying Bo's stomach in knots.

At last Dad shook his head, back and forth, back and forth, like an old person with that shaking disease. "I'm really sorry, Bo," he said. "But you've got to learn that the buck stops with you. What were you doing with your homework in your gym bag anyway? It belongs on your desk, doesn't it?"

Bo shrugged, and Dad pressed on. "You're twelve years old, for God's sake! Time you learned some responsibility. At far as I'm concerned, gymnastics is a privilege, something you earn. School is your job, and it has to come first."

Bo muttered that he wasn't twelve, not yet.

Dad eyed him sharply. "That'll be enough of that, young man. I'm sorry, Bozer. But if you get zeros on those two assignments tomorrow, I will have no choice but to keep you from competing on Sunday. It's that simple."

"Simple?" The word shot out of Bo's mouth louder than he'd expected. "You call that simple?"

"As far as I'm concerned, it is. You've got to stop blaming your problems on other people and own up to what you did wrong."

"But it *was* Jim's fault," Bo blurted. "He wants me out of the meet, don't you see? You're on *his* side! It's not fair!"

"I'm sorry," Dad said. "But I've got to stand firm on this."

"You don't *want* me to compete, do you? What's the matter? You got a meeting or something and can't watch me? I bet this is just an excuse." Bo rolled toward the wall and pulled the covers over his head. "I hope you know you're ruining my life. I thought we moved here to make things better."

"This has nothing to do with the move. Don't you see? I'd like nothing more than to watch you compete on Sunday. I really would. It's just that I don't know how else to teach you some responsibility. Taking away gymnastics is the only thing that'll make an impression." Dad stood up. "Try to get some sleep now. Tomorrow's school."

"Yeah, tomorrow's school all right."

Dad backed toward the door. "G'night, Bozer," he said, and closed it behind him.

"G'night, Bozer," Bo mimicked. *Good night? Ha!* It was the worst night of his life. Bo sat up, wadding his pillow in his lap. He pounded it with his fists, the way he felt like pounding Jim and Dad. "You're not going to beat me!" he whispered fiercely. "I won't let you!"

Tossing the pillow aside, Bo tiptoed to his desk. He took out his flashlight, his pony express note cards, a pencil, and some paper. Then he filled the crack under the door with his bedspread.

Yes, Dad, Bo thought. *Tomorrow's school. And I'm not going empty-handed.*

16

Second Thoughts

THE NEXT NIGHT at dinner Bo handed Dad a note from Mrs. Slater. She'd shown it to him only once, before break, but he knew it by heart: "Bo explained about the gym bag mix-up, and I am very proud of him for redoing his work and getting it in on time. I will grade the work he gave me today, but if his other work is better, I will give him the higher grade."

There! Bo thought. *That ought to show him.*

Dad fingered the note without reading it. "What's this?" he said. "Trouble at school?"

Bo pressed his lips together and sighed. "Just read it, will you?"

As he did, a grin spread across Dad's face. He passed the note to Mom and said, "See? If there's a will, there's a way. That's terrific, Bozer! I'm proud of you. How did you get everything done?''

"I stayed up until one."

"You did? In the dark?"

"Well, not exactly," Bo said, shoving his green beans away from his mashed potatoes. He didn't think Dad needed to know about the bedspread-under-the-door trick. "It's not as good as my other one was," he continued, "but I figured it was better than nothing."

"You figured right! Tell me something," Dad said. "Do you think you'd have done the work if I hadn't threatened to keep you out of the meet?"

Bo hesitated. It was a tricky question. Should he tell Dad the truth, or what he imagined the Perfect Son would say (and believe with all his heart): "Yes, Dad. Of course, I would have done the work if you hadn't threatened me." Never mind that the Perfect Son wouldn't have flubbed up in the first place. But then again, maybe the Perfect Son did not exist— and neither did the Perfect Father.

"I guess, um, probably not," Bo said at last, opting for the truth.

"I must admit, it *was* a pretty stiff consequence. But don't you feel better about yourself, taking responsibility like that?"

Bo squirmed. Somehow he didn't feel so proud anymore. He felt as if Dad were taking all the credit. "I guess," he said at last.

Dad seemed not to notice Bo's lack of conviction.

"Well," he said, slapping the table, "shall we get a sitter for Christopher on Sunday or go to the meet all together?"

"Get a sitter." Bo brightened. "Oh, Dad, that'd be perfect!" He jumped up to hug his father.

Christopher threw his spoon at Bo. He missed by a mile and hit the wall instead. "I wanna go to the meet," he said. "I wanna see my friend."

Bo rolled his eyes. He was sure Christopher meant Jim. "Don't spoil my dinner, Chris'per."

"You spoil *my* dinner," his brother replied.

"Well, you spoil my life!" Bo plopped into his chair, his arms folded across his chest. Why did Christopher have to go and mention Jim?

"Bo!" Mom glared at him across the table. "You apologize this minute. You hurt his feelings."

Christopher nodded. "You did, Bo. You made my feelings cry."

"Oh, for Pete's sake! Sor-ry." Bo shoveled the rest of his dinner down, except for the green beans, and asked to be excused.

"In a minute," Mom said. "Doesn't anyone want to hear *my* good news? I got a new account. The fitness center over on Odana. I'll be sewing dance wear for the boutique they just opened."

"What's dance wear?" Bo asked.

"Oh, you know. One-piece leotards, running tights. The best thing is, I can whip these up faster than the kids' smocks, and there's a bigger markup."

"That means more money for you, right?"

Mom reached across the table and ruffled his hair. "Right," she said. "Plus I get a free membership, *and* they have baby-sitting for Christopher."

"Sounds great, Nance," Dad said. "See? I knew everything would come together for you if you just gave it time."

"Way to go, Mom!" Bo chimed in. He couldn't believe it. All her problems solved at once. If only he could be so lucky at the Red Gym meet.

"Oh, Bo," Mom said, "one more thing. I thought you'd be glad to hear that your furniture finally came in. They'll deliver it on Monday."

"You mean it? But what about the room? There are boxes—"

"I know, I know. I promise," Mom said. "I'll clear everything out this weekend."

Bo rubbed his palms together with glee. "Oh, goody! My own room! At last!" He smiled pointedly at his brother.

Christopher stuck out his tongue. "My friend's going to beat you, Bo," he said. " 'Cuz he's nicer than you, that's why."

Bo scowled. He cleared his plate off the table and cleared out. *Jim's nicer? Ha!* He tried to push away the slow-motion replay of himself taking Jim's lucky grips. *That's different,* he thought. *I'm just teaching Jim a lesson.*

As he mounted the stairs, he could hear Mom

trying to talk Dad out of getting a sitter. It would be, she said, a nice family outing.

"Real nice," Bo muttered. Christopher would be there, rooting for Jim Harmon. Some brother. But then, what did he expect? Bo guessed he wasn't right up there vying for the Brother of the Year Award himself.

He went to their room to lay out his uniform for the meet. There were the grips, right where Bo had left them. At the bottom of Jim's old gym bag.

Bo closed the door and locked it. His heart was beating fast. He tried one of the grips on. It felt strange, like an alien skin that didn't quite fit. Ripping the Velcro free, he tossed the grip back into the bag and thought about what Christopher had said, that Jim was nicer. He did not want to believe it.

He thought about Jim's taking his bag and not returning it. Maybe the taking was an accident, but the not returning was definitely on purpose. Still, Bo had outfoxed him. The surprise would definitely be on Jim come Sunday. Bo could just imagine the look on Jim's face when he discovered his grips were gone.

He did not want to imagine past that moment. But his mind kept showing moving pictures behind his eyes: Jim was upset, searching everywhere for his grips. He was too upset to be angry, to think that Bo had taken them. The meet was starting and Jim looked like he was going to cry. He was really afraid that he wouldn't do well without those dumb little leather straps. . . .

Bo pressed his lips together and eyed Jim's grips. Taking them was definitely a creepy, not-nice thing to do, he decided. Probably worse than Jim's keeping his things and mailing his homework. Because in Jim's mind the lucky grips couldn't be replaced.

"I'm going to return them," he promised himself. "First thing on Sunday."

The day of the meet a stiff wind blustered off Lake Mendota. Bo, Mom, Dad, and Christopher fought against it all the way from the parking ramp to the University of Wisconsin's old Red Gym. It loomed before them on the shore like an ancient, redbrick castle.

Hot air from clanking radiators greeted them. They followed the crowd upstairs to the gym.

Bo's eyes widened. The place was huge! There were old skylights above and tall windows everywhere that flooded the gym with sunshine. The right wall was lined with wooden bleachers, except for one corner, where the booster club was selling T-shirts, snacks, and coffee.

Dad and Christopher made a beeline for the doughnuts. Bo spied Jack and Stu and a couple of the guys sitting on the floor-exercise mat. He wove his way toward them. Mom was tagging right behind.

Bo scanned the gym, certain he was the only gymnast with a mother for a shadow. "Why don't you go find some seats?" he said. "I'll be all right."

"You sure?"

Bo nodded. "I'll be up to drop my stuff off in a while, okay?"

Mom surveyed the crowd. "I'll be over there by that blond woman. I think I've seen her before at Capital."

Bo squinted, following her finger halfway up the center section near the aisle. "That's Taysa! See? I told you you knew her."

Jim's mother was cuddled up to a silver-haired man with a neck as big as a tree trunk. Jim's dad, probably. He certainly did resemble the gold-chain guy they'd seen in Sampson's. But from this distance, Bo couldn't be sure.

Someone was waving wildly in Bo's direction. It was Matthew. He and his parents were sitting nearby. Bo waved back.

"Why don't you go sit by the Weilers?" Bo said, thinking about Jim's lucky grips. There had to be a better day for Mom to get friendly with Taysa Harmon.

Mom shrugged. "What difference does it make?"

Bo sighed in exasperation.

"Oh, all right. I'll sit with the Weilers."

Bo watched her shuffle off, then turned back toward his team. As he did, he saw Jim charging toward him. Jim's eyebrows made one angry slash across his forehead.

Bo gulped and tried to sidestep him. But Jim grabbed the sleeve of his sweatshirt and pulled him back.

17

Decisions, Decisions

"WHAT ARE *YOU* DOING HERE?" Jim demanded. "I thought your dad said—"

"I know what he said," Bo snapped. "What's it to you?"

"Wouldn't you like to know." Jim's eyes darted up into the stands and back again.

"Actually," Bo said, "I couldn't care less." Jim *had* done it on purpose. He was just like Mickey Schrader, through and through. Jerking free of Jim's grasp, Bo stormed off across the mat. No way was he going to return Jim's grips now. The guy deserved to squirm.

Jim fell into step beside Bo. "Forget the gold, Ragatz," he hissed. "It's gonna be mine. It's . . ." Jim's voice trailed off. He mumbled something to himself. It sounded like "gotta be."

Bo tried to ignore him. He checked in with Jack, then started stretching out with the other guys.

A half hour later, the meet announcer divided the fourteen teams into six groups. He told them on which apparatus they would begin their timed warm-ups. Bo knew that the groups would have only ten minutes to get used to each piece of equipment before the meet began.

"Go put your bags away," Jack said, "and hustle over to high bar. The clock's ticking."

High bar. Jim would be looking for his grips.

Bo ran up into the bleachers ahead of Jim. He greeted the Weilers and Matthew, then thrust the bag at Mom. Dad and Christopher had joined her and were finishing the last of their doughnuts.

Bo glanced nervously over at Jim's parents. They were in the next row up, directly behind Matthew. His suspicions about the gold-chain guy from Sampson's were correct. Poor Jim. His dad looked old enough to be his grandfather.

Several teenaged girls were crowded behind Taysa, getting her autograph. Jim's dad looked amused at first. But as the gathering grew, he seemed annoyed. At last he turned around and said something, and Taysa's admirers faded into the stands.

Someone tapped Bo's arm. "Good luck, honey," Mom was saying. "Just do your best. That's good enough. Don't worry about winning, okay?"

Good old Mom. Bo nodded, wondering whether

she too had recognized Mr. Harmon from the sporting-goods store. Probably not. She was too busy fussing over Bo. Grudgingly, he accepted her kiss on the cheek.

"Mom's right," Dad added. "Just go out there and have fun."

"I'm saving you a brownie," Christopher said. He held his fist out. Chocolate frosting oozed between his fingers.

Bo made a face. "Thanks, Chris'per. But you can have it."

Christopher's face lit up. "I can? Oh, goody! I hope you win, Bo."

"Really?" Somehow, Bo realized, that meant a lot.

"Really!" Christopher grinned up at him. Bo marveled at how forgiving the kid was. Either that or he had a short memory.

As Bo turned to go, Jim passed behind Mom and Dad. He shoved his gold gym bag at his mother and asked her to get out his grips.

Bo gulped. He couldn't move, though everything in him wanted to flee.

"Bo! Hey, psst!" Matthew was waving him over.

Bo managed to unglue his feet and inch past the Weilers. Matthew seemed a million miles away.

"I can't find them," Taysa was saying. A new group of autograph seekers had stolen up behind her, waving napkins and scraps of papers over her shoulder. Taysa sighed, plastered a sticky smile on, and asked them to please come back later.

Jim scowled as the girls slunk off. "Look again, Mom," he ordered. "I know they're there. I put them away right after practice."

"Jamey, they're not here," she said.

Jim pounded one fist into his other open hand. "You look, Dad," he said. "I'm going to lose without them!"

"You are not," Mr. Harmon said. "Grips or no grips, you're going to win, do you hear me?"

"W-what if I don't?" Jim's voice sounded like a little kid's.

Bo wished he were invisible. He slunk down beside Matthew, touching his finger to his lips. Matthew nodded.

"You'll win," Taysa said. "All those private lessons we paid for? How could you not?" Out of the corner of his eye, Bo could see her rubbing a smudge of chalk dust off Jim's skinny gold step-in strap. Like they'd take off points. Like the judges even cared.

"B-but what if I don't?"

"James!" His dad sounded annoyed. "Just concentrate and remember your knees and toes."

"Knees and toes," Jim repeated, bobbing his head lamely. "But what about my grips?"

"Bo," Matthew whispered, "did you—"

Bo clapped his hand over Matthew's mouth.

Matthew's eyes widened as they met Bo's. He mouthed the question, "Really?"

Bo gave a slight nod.

"I'm glad *I'm* on your good side," Matthew mumbled, almost to himself.

"What's that supposed to mean?"

Matthew shrugged. "I *did* mess up the math test for you."

"Oh, that." Bo waved away Matthew's concern. "That's different."

Matthew just blinked at him.

"Really," Bo said. "It is."

Matthew shrugged. "If you say so."

"I do. Wish me luck?"

"Yeah," Matthew said. "That's what I was going to say before . . ." He looked over his shoulder. "I think you're going to need it. In more ways than one."

Bo nodded and headed toward the high bar. He tried not to think about Jim or the lucky grips. Winning. That's what he was here for, no matter what Mom and Dad said. And Jim Harmon was not going to stop him.

Bo glanced back up at Matthew. He couldn't believe it! Matthew was talking to Jim! Bo gulped. Surely Matthew wouldn't be ratting. They were friends, for Pete's sake. But what had Matthew meant about being glad to be on Bo's good side?

"Hey, Ragatz!" Jack called. "Shake a leg, will you? Time's wasting."

Bo managed to squeeze in a turn on the high bar before the teams had to rotate. But Jim didn't catch up until they were already on floor exercise, getting used to the spring floor.

"Jack, I can't find my grips!" Jim panted. "I've looked everywhere, but they're gone." Bo had never seen him look so out of control. He was ready to cry or explode—Bo didn't know which.

Jack slipped an arm around Jim's shoulders and tried to calm him down. "Trust me," he said, "you'll get by just fine with plain old chalk."

Bo's heart was thudding so loudly, he was sure they'd hear and guess his secret. At least Matthew hadn't told. That was a relief, for the moment, anyway. Afraid to hang around and listen, Bo stuck with Stu and threw a couple of back handsprings.

At last timed warm-ups were over. One by one the teams were announced, marched out, and lined up on the floor-exercise mat. Denny, because he was shortest, led the Capital boys. Bo stood behind him.

Then everyone rose for "The Star-Spangled Banner."

"O'er the land of the free and the home of the brave," Bo sang.

Brave? *That's a laugh,* he thought. *I'm not even brave enough to return Jim's grips.*

The announcer called out the rotations. Capital

and the Twin City Twisters proceeded to the vault area.

Bo sat down to await his turn. Jed and Eric plopped down on either side. Eric's arms were covered with chalk dust from the warm-ups. He looked like a ghost. The other guys—Pete, Dave, Andy, and Tony—squeezed onto the mat behind them, while Denny busied himself at the chalk bucket. Jim was pacing back and forth, shooting worried glances at his parents up in the stands. As Phil Bender ambled by, Jim tapped his arm.

"Phil, I know you hate me," he said, "but please, I've gotta know if you've seen my grips."

"You think I took them?"

"I didn't say that." Jim drew his fingers through his wavy hair. "It's just . . . well, you *would* tell me if you'd seen them, wouldn't you?"

"Sure. Why not?"

Phil stood against the wall with the taller guys from the Twin City Twisters. Jim started pacing again. Bo moved around, trying to lose himself among Dave, Pete, Tony, and the others. He didn't want Jim asking him the same questions. Finally, Jack called him to vault.

After the judge's nod, Bo charged toward the horse, pumping his arms and leaning well forward. He hit the board dead center and reached for the leather, his body knifing through the air. The elevation was good!

He squatted over. The postflight felt great! He sank his heels deep into the mat, sticking his landing.

The judge flashed a 9.0.

"Good start," Bo told himself as he jogged back to rejoin his team.

Soon it was Jim's turn. He looked like he was running in slow motion. His vault lacked its usual height and distance. The judge gave him an 8.3.

Again Jim looked up into the stands. His father motioned him sharply. A moment later, Jim was dashing up there.

Bo wished he could hear what Mr. Harmon was saying. Mr. Harmon was holding fast to Jim's shoulders, and his jowls shook. Jim hung his head and finally trudged back toward the team. He sat by himself, hugging his legs against his chest.

Bo almost felt sorry for him. But there wasn't time. They had to rotate to parallel bars. And he had to keep his mind on what he was doing.

Remembering how rough the wooden bars had felt during warm-ups, he chalked his upper arms so they wouldn't chafe. Then he examined his palms. One of his calluses looked a little puffy, as if maybe it had blistered.

Bo shook his head, banished the thought. He hadn't had a rip since they'd moved to Wisconsin. The last thing he needed was one right now. After chalking his hands, he rubbed his nose with the back of his wrist, then signaled the judge.

With the nod, Bo hit the board and jumped to an upper-arm support. When he cast to his back uprise, he could feel his legs swing back higher than usual. Maybe he'd get a tenth of a point for virtuosity! His L-support was solid; he knew his legs didn't dip below the bars.

Steady now, he told himself as he straddle-pressed to his shoulder stand. He ignored the aching pressure of the bars against his joints.

As he rolled forward and continued swinging through the rest of the routine, his heart was pounding with excitement. He just knew it was good!

The judge flashed a 9.2. Jack tousled his hair as he returned to the mat. *If Ruiz were here,* Bo thought, *he would have done more than that.* He pushed the twinge of disappointment away and mentally tallied his scores.

Jim was up next. Bo held his breath as Jim began his routine. His legs fell slightly on his L and his shoulder stand lacked its usual form and polish. There was no amplitude in his swings.

When he saw that his score was a whole point lower than Bo's, Jim's bottom lip quivered. His eyes looked red and shiny.

Bo noticed Taysa coming down from the bleachers. The zillion gold chains nestling on her sweater flashed beneath the overhead lights. When she reached the edge of the floor-ex mat, she just stood there, staring past Jim at the judge. *No way she can charm a higher score out of him,* Bo thought, *if that's what she's trying to do.* Her carefully painted lips parted slightly, as if she wanted to tell Jim something but decided not to. Then several google-eyed girls encircled her, waving slips of paper in her face. And she was there, but she was gone.

A strange lump lodged itself in Bo's throat. He tried to choke it down. But it would not budge. He tried to ignore it. But it would not go away. Maybe Mom and Dad *weren't* perfect. But at least they were there for *him.* Which was different from Jim's parents, who were there only for themselves.

Yeah, our folks are different all right, Bo thought, remembering Jim's wistful comparison of mothers that day at practice: "Different's not better." Isn't that what he'd said? And hadn't Bo thought he was crazy?

Now, as Bo glanced over at Jim, he realized that Jim had been telling the truth. *His* truth, anyway. Different *wasn't* better . . . for *him.* But it was for Bo. By a long shot.

The Winner

"I'LL BE RIGHT BACK," Bo whispered to Jed. He took off across the mat, nudged past Taysa and her fans, and hurried up the steps to where his parents were sitting.

"Mom, quick!" he panted. "Give me the gym bag!"

Bewildered, she handed it over, and Bo began shoving his shoes and clothes at her.

"What's all this?" she asked.

"Never mind. Just . . . thanks."

As he flung the bag over his shoulder, Taysa brushed past him, her face lined with annoyance. "I wish he'd get it together," she said to her husband. "I'm so exhausted, I'd just as soon go home and rest up for that shoot in Jamaica."

Bo glanced back at her again as he raced toward

the parallel bars. Somehow she didn't seem quite so beautiful. Not anymore.

His usually dry palms began to sweat as he approached Jim. "Here," he said, extending the bag.

Jim scowled. "What do I want with that?"

Bo stared at a rip in the thick, blue landing mat. "Look inside," he said quietly.

Jim unzipped the bag. "Hey! My grips!"

Bo turned to go. But Jim caught his arm.

Bo whirled about. He tensed every muscle, ready for Jim's attack. Instead Jim demanded, "How'd *you* get 'em?"

Bo swallowed hard. "I-I found them," he said, half-truthfully. His courage waned. He couldn't quite muster the words *in your other gym bag.* "Lucky for you, huh?"

Jim said nothing. He cocked his head, regarding Bo queerly. At last he cleared his throat. "Thanks, Bo. I-I really mean it, too."

Bo let the words sink in slowly. "Yeah," he said, "I'm sure you do." Now Jim had no excuse for messing up.

Jim looked up at his parents, waving his grips back and forth above his head. Mr. Harmon gave him the thumbs-up sign. Jim extended his hand to Bo.

Bo blinked in disbelief. Jim hadn't guessed the truth! He wasn't angry! Hesitantly, Bo extended his own and shook. Jim's hand was as slippery as a wet bar of soap.

"No wonder you need grips," Bo said, wiping the sweat on his white pants.

Jim grinned. "It only gets this bad when I have an audience." He nodded toward his parents.

Bo followed Jim's gaze. Even though it was between events, Taysa and Mr. Harmon were watching him as if he were an insect under their microscope. Dad, on the other hand, was reading Christopher a book that Mom had tucked into her purse. And Mom was making notes on a clipboard.

"Know what I mean?" Jim asked.

Bo nodded glumly. He knew all right. The difference between their parents' attitudes was enough to make anyone sweat. "Hey, Jim," he said, "good luck, huh?"

"Thanks! I'm going to need it after my last two scores." Jim wriggled into his grips as the announcer called for the teams to rotate. Capital would be on high bar next.

Bo turned back to rejoin Jed and Eric.

"Hey, Shrim— Oops! I mean, Bo," Jim called after him. "You'd better watch out for me now!"

Bo stopped in midstride. *What?* he thought. *No more Shrimpboat? This is too good to be true!*

Jack hustled the team over to the high bar. Eric and Jed kept asking Bo what was going on with him and Harmon.

Bo just shrugged. It wasn't the kind of thing he

wanted to put into words. At least, not yet. It was too new, too shaky.

Bo turned his thoughts to the high bar and to the other events he had yet to perform—floor, pommels, and rings. Judging from the other scores he'd seen so far, hitting high eights and low nines would give him a good chance at the gold.

Sandwiched between Eric and Jed, Bo sat on the mat, awaiting his turn. Jim was pacing back and forth. For once, he was ignoring his parents.

"Hey, Harmon," Tony said, "you found your grips! Way to go!"

Jim mustered a quick smile but no explanation and returned to his pacing.

Bo was up fifth. He examined his now angry-red blister and coated his palms with chalk. "Please don't rip," he whispered.

Jack lifted him up to the pipe. He cast forward and up, his toes aimed at the ceiling. On the backswing he released the bar, flew free for a moment, and regrasped it on the way down. His legs were taut, his toes pointed.

As he completed his single-leg shoot and kip to a stride support, he reminded himself about continuity. Each pause, each hesitation could mean a three-tenths deduction.

He took care not to overrotate on his back hip circle. Just as he was swinging under the bar for the straight body–shoot dismount, he felt one hand slip. In the same instant, a sharp pain burned through his palm. A rip!

Bo gritted his teeth, tried to recover. He released the bar with relief. His distance and height felt good. Now to nail it . . . almost. The thickness of the mat altered his balance, and he landed with one step to the side. *Oh, well,* he thought. *It could have been worse.*

He saluted the judge, then examined his palm. As he awaited his score, he blew on the raw circle of red skin. Despite the landing, the judge decided on a 9.2.

The guys clapped and congratulated him. But Jim did not come over. For an instant, his eyes met Bo's. He offered a fleeting smile, then chalked up. It was his turn next.

Bo held his breath as Jim fiddled with his grips. Now the guy had no excuse. *But will he be able to pull out of his slump?* Bo wondered.

Jim rocketed forward and up from his hanging position. He seemed propelled by an inner fire. His release and regrasp were so daring that Bo thought he wouldn't connect. But he did, and continued pumping higher. His underswings were way above horizontal—great virtuosity!

Bo shook his head in disbelief. The guy was amazing. On the dismount, Jim arched so high that his hips came above the bar. And it seemed only right that after a routine like that, he stuck his landing as well.

The judge agreed, awarding him a 9.6.

This time Bo led the applause, but winced as he clapped his hands. Jim blushed at all the attention.

Next they moved on to floor exercise. Jack had Jim precede Bo in the lineup. They wriggled out of their long white pants, changed into shorts, and limbered up on a nearby tumbling mat.

Taysa was cheering Jim on, but Jim seemed not to notice. His eyes were fixed on the far corner of the spring floor as he exploded into his first tumbling pass.

All his tricks were clicking. They flowed smoothly, and Bo couldn't spot even a minor form break. Jim was closing the point spread.

Bo's pulse quickened as he read Jim's score. 9.5! If Bo wanted to stay in the lead, he'd need an 8.3 or better. *Of all the times to get a rip.*

With the judge's nod, Bo started his routine from a different corner, just as he'd done during the intersquad meet. The mat scraped against his raw palm on the handstand. His balance shifted, affecting his hold.

Forget it, go on, he told himself, concentrating on flow and form as he moved into his cartwheel-chassé combination.

His heart was thudding against the mat as he eased

into his pancake. He knew at once he'd held the position too long. Another deduction! *Darn!*

Bo rolled back onto his shoulders, but leaned slightly to one side. He tensed his muscles, trying to save the trick. *Whew!* At least he could recover! He eased to his feet, moving smoothly into his front scale. *Head and chest up! Toe pointed! Leg turned out! Nice and steady.*

Then, with a quick intake of breath, he shot forward into his hurdle, round off, and back handspring. He punched the floor on his final straight jump, gaining good elevation and landing under control.

He pressed his lips together, fuming silently at his 8.5.

"That's nothing to sneeze at," Jack said. "Your balance was a little off. That's all."

Balance! Bo chided himself. Maybe that's what Jim was doing with all this nice-guy stuff. Trying to throw him off balance. Hadn't Bo learned anything from Mickey Schrader? He should have known to expect the unexpected.

"Think it'd help to tape my rip?" Bo asked.

"Couldn't hurt," Jack said. "Here. Let me see it."

Bo offered the coach his palm. Jack wrapped it with adhesive tape.

Pommel horse, the next event, was definitely not the place to pad his lead, Bo thought. He'd be lucky not to fall off. Especially now, with his rip.

Bo gritted his teeth as his hands gripped the pommels. He counted silently to himself, pacing his leg cuts and side travels. His arms were shaking. He feared his elbows might give way at any second.

But somehow he made it to the dismount and scissored off with glee. He was so relieved to have pommels behind him, his 8.8 felt like a gift.

Jim bit his lip, but his eyes danced with hope. Bo was sure he was thinking that this was his big chance, and he attacked the side horse as if to prove who was boss. His long legs cleared the leather and swept upward in an even rhythm. He made it look easy.

Bo gulped at Jim's 9.1. Now they were tied!

The announcer called the last rotation. Jim strapped his grips on again, this time for the still rings. Bo tried to ignore Jim's pacing. It was making his stomach bounce around like Jell-O. Why couldn't the guy just sit down like everyone else?

Jack told Bo to chalk up. As he dipped his hands in the soft powder, Jim came up from behind.

"I know you took my grips, Bo," he whispered.

Oh, please, Bo thought, *don't get into this now!* He clapped the extra chalk off and said nothing.

"What I mean is," Jim continued, "I don't blame you."

Bo turned around, blinking with surprise. "You don't?"

Jim shook his head. "I guess I had it coming."

"Yeah, well, it was a dumb thing for me to do. I'm sorry."

"You know," Jim said, "I don't get it. You could have beaten me for sure if you hadn't given them back."

"Yeah, maybe I could've. But it wouldn't mean anything. Not like that."

Jim grinned. "Lucky for me." He tapped Bo's wrist. "You know, your rip would feel a lot better if you had grips." He paused. "You want to use mine?"

"You'd let *me* use your lucky grips? Do you mean it?"

Jim nodded. He ripped the grips free and plopped them into Bo's hand.

"Jim, hey, this is really nice of you!" Bo fingered the leather straps hesitantly and remembered the time he'd tried them on in his room. They still felt strange, like somehow they just didn't belong on his hands. Despite his rip, Bo handed them back. "Thanks, really," he said. "But I think I'll be okay."

"Suit yourself." Jim shrugged. "And, uh . . . good luck." It sounded like he really meant it.

Bo took his place under the rings and closed his eyes for a moment, trying to visualize his routine. But all he could think about was the stupid war between him and Jim. It was over! It was finally over! Bo felt as if he could jump all the way up to those high rings without help.

He pulled smoothly to his straight body–inverted hang, piked, and swung forward into his inlocates.

He tensed his stomach muscles and managed to make them straight body. All that practice had paid off. His L-hang was solid, his swings high and controlled.

Now for the dislocate! Bo flung the rings out at the height of the swing and continued into his tuck flyaway dismount. He spotted the mat, bent his knees, and let them absorb the impact of his landing. He sank down, straining to keep his balance. Slowly he lifted his arms and threw his chest out in triumph.

The judge flashed a 9.2, his best rings score ever. Now it was Jim's turn.

Bo was so excited and nervous, he could hardly breathe. He watched Jim pull to his inverted hang with straight body and arms. *Did I do that, too?* Bo wondered.

Jim's backward swings were well above the horizontal. He was going to get a 10 if he kept this up. Bo's heart was thrumming in his throat. Jim's routine was good. Very good. But was it better than Bo's? Bo crossed his fingers and waited. At last came the score—9.2, the same as Bo's.

"We tied!" Bo said.

"Maybe." Jim smiled mysteriously as he ripped his grips off. "Then again, maybe not."

"What's that supposed to mean?"

"You'll see," Jim replied. "Hey! Here comes your brother!"

Bo followed Jim's pointing finger. Sure enough,

there was Christopher, running toward them across the mat. And some guy from Salto was right in the middle of a floor-ex routine.

"Oh, no!" Bo groaned. "I *told* them to leave him with a baby-sitter."

Jim laughed as he crouched down and held his arms out.

"Go ahead and laugh," Bo said. "It's easy for you. He's not *your* brother."

"Well, he's gotta be better than no brother at all."

"You really think so?"

"Absolutely," Jim said. "At least you have someone to play with."

"Play with?"

Jim shrugged. "Fight with. It's all the same, isn't it?"

Bo didn't know what to say. He watched Christopher jump up and wrap his legs around Jim's waist. His brother looked kind of cute, like one of those clip-on bears.

Bo fought off a stab of jealousy. He wanted to tell Christopher that he was there, too. But he didn't. Couldn't. Maybe later he'd find the right words. Maybe tomorrow. When he moved into his own room.

Christopher stuck tight to Jim through the last of the floor-exercise routines. Then he sat down on the mat with all the gymnasts to await the awards ceremony. Bo could feel his stomach knotting up.

It seemed like forever before the announcer was ready to call off the twelve winners in the ten-to-twelve age group. First he handed out medals to the thirteen-to-fifteens. Pete Carboni finished fourth, while Phil Bender missed a gold medal by two-tenths. Jed Lewis placed tenth, and Eric Weiler twelfth. In the seven-to-nine age group, Andy Thayer finished third, and Denny Spencer tied for eleventh. Bo could hardly breathe.

At last the announcer awarded ribbons in the ten-to-twelve age group to the guys in fourth through twelfth place. Tony Myers was unlucky thirteenth.

The bronze, third-place medal went to a kid from Fox Valley. He had scored 51.9.

"We have a tie for second between James Harmon and Bo Ragatz, both from Capital Gymnastics Academy," the announcer said. "But in the event of a tie, first place goes to the gymnast with the highest individual score."

Jim peeled Christopher off his lap. He and Bo approached the platform.

"So, in second place is Bo Ragatz and in first is James Harmon with a fifty-three-point-nine. Congratulations, boys!"

Someone slipped a silver medal on a red, white, and blue ribbon around Bo's neck. He jumped up onto the second-place step. Flashbulbs exploded from the bleachers. Bo waved at Mom and Dad and

Matthew . . . and even at Christopher. Then he studied the shiny medal on his chest.

Pictured there were three gymnasts, one on rings, another on pommels, and the third on P bars. Except for the color, it was the same as Jim's.

Silver. Gold. What is the difference, really? Bo wondered.

He turned to Jim, extending his hand. Instead of taking it, Jim grabbed his wrist and pulled him up onto the top step. It was so crowded that Bo had to stick to Jim's side to keep from falling off.

"Just thought you'd like to be taller," Jim said, his eyes laughing.

"Me? Taller?" Bo looked up at Jim and grinned. *Looking up isn't the worst thing in the world,* he thought. *Especially when that's what things are starting to do—at last!*

Information on Competitive Boys' Gymnastics

Under the auspices of the United States Gymnastics Federation (for information, write to: 201 South Capitol, Pan American Plaza, Suite 300, Indianapolis, IN 46225; or call 317-237-5050), boys' gymnastics competition is divided into *age groups* (7–9, 10–12, 13–15, 16–18) and *classes,* which reflect a gymnast's level of ability.

Class IV, in which Bo and his team compete, is considered an advanced beginner level. When a gymnast performs especially well in one class, he is moved up to the next class at the end of the competitive season. Before competing, he must learn more difficult routines on each apparatus. Bo and Jim, for example, would compete next year in *Class III.* And since Jim would turn thirteen in the interim, he would also move into an older age group.

In Class IV competition, all boys perform the same routines. These are called *compulsories* and are changed by the USGF after the Olympics every four years. Beginning with Class III, boys who wish to and are able may also create their own routines for each apparatus. These are called *optionals*. A gymnast who elects to perform optionals must compete in compulsories as well. Few boys under the age of ten have the strength and skill to compete in Class III.

The boys' competitive season usually runs from fall until late spring. Most teams practice year-round. Meets may be as simple as a practice intersquad meet, or they may involve twenty to thirty teams from around the state or region.

The Olympic order of events is floor exercise, pommel horse, still rings, vault, parallel bars, and high bar. Because many teams compete during an invitational meet, such as the Red Gym meet, they are usually divided into six groups. In this way, all six apparatuses are in constant use. A team may begin competition on vault, for example, but rotations still proceed in Olympic order, ending with still rings.

Glossary of Gymnastics Terms

*AMPLITUDE   Refers to movements being of full measure or maximum performance of the skill; exaggerated or expanded to the fullest.

*ARCH   A basic position in which the back is curved backward (hyperextended) and the hips and knees are extended.

BACK EXTENSION ROLL   A tumbling move in which the gymnast rolls in a backward direction and pushes, or extends, into a handstand before the feet touch the floor.

*BOARD, REUTHER BOARD   The official take-off springboard for the vaulting event. It may also be used for mounting the parallel bars.

*BREAK   An error of execution during a perfor-

144

mance. Judges recognize minor breaks (point deductions of 0.1–0.3) and major breaks (point deductions according to the seriousness of the error).

*CAST   To thrust the body in a given direction by means of a forceful hip extension from a pike position. Example: *cast* to a high underswing on the horizontal bar.

*CHALK (magnesium carbonate)   A powdery substance that the gymnast places on his hands in order to insure a firm grip on the apparatus. Chalk absorbs the excess moisture on the palms of the hands.

*CHASSÉ (pronounced "shaw-SAY")   A dance step in which one foot chases the other.

*COMPULSORY EXERCISE   The competitive gymnastic routine or vault that every performer in each class is required to execute.

*CONTINUITY   The term used to refer to the togetherness of a routine or skill. A routine is said to possess this quality if it has been performed without unnecessary pauses or movements that do not appear to belong together.

*CUT   The passage of one or both legs between the hands and the apparatus. A gymnast may perform a single-leg cut with either leg, a joined cut with both legs together under one hand, or a straddle cut with both legs passing out to the sides (laterally) under both hands.

DISLOCATE A backward rotating skill performed from a hang on the still rings.

*DISMOUNT (or **dismount combination**) The last skill or series of skills in a routine, executed prior to the landing on the floor.

*ELEVATION The height achieved by a performer on dismounts, vaults, and tumbling skills.

*EXECUTION The technical manner in which a skill is performed. The standard has been set by tradition, with a small margin of originality allowable.

*EXERCISE, ROUTINE A planned series of skills a gymnast performs in a given event.

FLASH (as in "flash scores" or "flasher") Showing a gymnast's scores by writing them on a blackboard or flipping numbers on a specially designed board.

*FLEXIBILITY Relates to the individual gymnast's range of movement in various joint areas.

FLYAWAY A dismount involving a backward, airborne flip, performed in a tuck, pike, or layout position, with a landing on one's feet.

*FORM Refers to the technique of keeping the

limbs straight, or straight and together, or tucked according to conventional gymnastics standards.

*GRIPS, HAND GUARDS   A piece of leather or fiber that fits over the fingers, covers the palms, and attaches to the wrists. The hand guard protects the palm of the hand from friction created by swinging on the apparatus.

*HANG, SUSPENSION   To support the body by the hands, arms, or legs with most of the body below the point of support.

*HOLD   Refers to a stationary position, such as an L or a scale, that is used on the parallel bars, rings, or floor-exercise events. In all events the position is held for two seconds.

*HURDLE   A method of leaping from one foot to two feet. It is used in tumbling and vaulting as a means of converting a run into a two-footed landing in preparation for a powerful jump.

INLOCATE   A forward rotating skill performed from a hang on the still rings.

*INVERTED   A straight up-and-down (vertical) position with the body held upside down, as in an inverted hang.

KIP   A skill in which the gymnast maneuvers from a hanging position below the apparatus to a supported position above it.

LAYOUT, STRAIGHT BODY The body position in which the hips, knees, and back are held in a straight line and extended.

*L-HANG, L-SUPPORT A position in which the legs are held parallel with the floor and the upper body is held in a straight-up (vertical) position.

*MOUNT The first skill or series of skills that the gymnast uses to start his exercise. On the side horse (pommel horse) and parallel bars, the mount starts from a stand or jump. On the rings and horizontal bar, the mount starts from a hang. In the floor-exercise event, the mount is considered to be the first skill or series of skills performed. This term does not apply to the vaulting event.

NAIL IT See *Stick the dismount.*

*OPTIONALS Routines composed of skills of the gymnast's own choice.

PANCAKE A colloquial expression used to describe a tumbling flexibility move in which the gymnast's legs are in a wide straddle as he leans forward and touches his upper body to the floor, with his hips coming as close to the floor as possible.

*PIKE A standard position for executing various skills, in which the knees are straight and the hips are flexed as much as the gymnast's flexibility will allow.

*POSTFLIGHT The period after the hands leave the floor or the horse up to the point of landing on the feet during handspring movements.

*PREFLIGHT The period of flight after the feet leave the floor in tumbling (or the board in vaulting) up to the point when the hands contact the floor (or the horse) during handspring movements.

*REVERSE To execute a given movement in the opposite direction from the established one.

*RIP, TEAR A torn blister or patch of skin on the palm of the hand.

ROUND-OFF–BACK HANDSPRING A tumbling combination featuring a round-off (similar to a cartwheel but with a half-twist into a two-footed landing) that leads immediately into a back handspring.

*SCALE A held position used in floor exercise, characterized by a balance on one foot with the other leg and arms placed according to the particular type of scale.

*SHOOT To extend the hips, with the legs leading, in order to give the body impetus in a given direction. A gymnast may shoot up, on, or over the apparatus, between or outside the grips.

*SINGLE LEG Skills that are performed with the legs separated and that emphasize the use of one leg.

*SPOTTING   Refers to the system of aiding the gymnast during the performance of various skills. An individual may be spotted by hand (without additional equipment) or with a safety belt.

*SQUAT   Action of bending the trunk and the knees to the floor. This term is often used to describe a similar action of the trunk, hips, and knees while the body is supported on the hands.

STEP-IN   The sleeveless leotardlike uniform boys wear in competition. White shorts are worn over it for vault and floor exercises. Long, white stretch pants are worn over it for rings, parallel bars, pommel horse, and horizontal bar.

STICK THE DISMOUNT   A solid landing after the final series of skills (as if both feet are "stuck" to the mat). Ideally, the landing should have no hops or missteps. Also referred to as *nailing it.*

STILL RINGS   The set of two wooden rings suspended either from a beam in the gym's ceiling or from a metal structure (called a *ring tower*), on which gymnasts perform a series of skills. During use, the rings are to remain as still as possible, and points are deducted accordingly.

*STRADDLE   Sideways (lateral) spreading of the legs.

*SUPPORT   A position in which the body is supported by the arms with the shoulders held above the point of support.

*SWING A movement in which the body follows a circular pathway while supported on or hanging from the apparatus. Learning to swing with control is one of the beginner's first tasks.

*TIMING Control of the speed and coordination of a movement in order that it may reach its maximum at a given moment.

*TRAVEL A term applied to the skills that move the gymnast from one area of the apparatus to another. This term usually refers to a group of skills on the pommel horse.

*TUCK A maximum flexion of the hips and knees. The back is usually rounded forward and the hands grasp the lower legs just below the knee joint. Most somersaulting skills are taught in this position before the pike or layout position is attempted.

*VAULT A jump over the vaulting horse in which one or both hands touch the horse. This term also applies to certain mounts on the parallel bars that require a jump over one bar.

VIRTUOSITY This term refers to a single skill or a series of skills performed together with unusual talent for artistic execution. Points given for virtuosity can elevate a "perfect" routine past 9.6 and edge it toward 10.

*WARM-UP   The series of formal and/or informal exercises that prepare the body for training or performing on the gymnastic apparatuses. The gymnastic warm-up usually involves flexibility exercises, jogging, and formal movements on a chosen apparatus.

* Taken or paraphrased with permission
from **GYMNASTICS ILLUSTRATED**
Copyright © 1972 by Don Tonry
Gymnastic Aides
Box 475, Northbridge, Massachusetts